MISPRINT

HOMECOMING

GALLOWGLASS #3

JENNIFER ALLIS PROVOST

CONTENTS

MISPRINT

GOING HOME

"I still do no' think traveling by air is necessary," Robert said. "'Tis unnatural."

I glanced at Robert. At six feet three inches tall with the body of a warrior, he didn't look like a man who was afraid of flying, but looks can be deceiving. "How else do you propose we cross the Atlantic?" I asked.

"We should make the crossing aboard a ship, as people were meant to," he declared.

I rolled my eyes; this wasn't the first discussion we'd had about air travel. "That would take forever."

"Actually, it would take less than a week," my brother, Chris, said. The three of us were in the airport waiting to board our flight from New York to Scotland. We had spent the past few weeks recovering from our run-in with some Greek gods, and getting ready to move back to our cottage in Crail. After everything we'd been through this past winter, I was more than ready to start over across the sea.

Robert and I were starting over in more ways than one: we were having a baby. The baby was unplanned, unexpected, and the most wonderful thing that had ever happened. We'd already named her Faith, and I couldn't wait to meet her.

"Most ships departing from New York dock in Glasgow or Edinburgh in about six days," Chris continued.

I glared at him. There was no way I was taking my morning sickness on a six-day cruise. "Well, since we already bought the plane tickets, it looks like we're flying. Have you heard from Anya?"

"She sent me a message this morning," Chris replied. Anya was Chris's girlfriend. She also happened to be the daughter of Beira, the legendary Cailleach Bheur and the Celtic Queen of Winter, because us Stewart kids just can't manage to hook up with regular humans. In addition to her impressive lineage, Anya also had the ability to teleport, which meant she would miss out on questionable airplane food and cramped middle seats. "She's already at the cottage with Wyatt," Chris added.

Wyatt was the leader of the wights—butterfly-sized fairies that watched over gardens—and he and the rest of his flock lived at our cottage in Crail, a tiny seaside village in Scotland. Yep, Robert and I owned property in Scotland, and how we came by that is a long story indeed.

We'd spent the last six months in New York, mainly so I could finish up my doctorate in geology and Chris could clean up some legal troubles. I'd expected a quiet few months, but instead I learned that my mentor was actually Demeter—yeah, the Greek goddess—and that she was starting a cult at our school. Then Robert got attacked by centaurs and sent to a hell dimension to battle the Hydra, Hades slapped a *geas* on Demeter, and Chris gave up his teaching career to be with the aforementioned Anya. So yeah, we were going back to Scotland.

Our time in New York hadn't been all bad. I'd learned the Mama Anastasia, the sweet older lady who ran the diner near my apartment, was Persephone in disguise. She and her son, Andreas, had helped us defeat her mother. She'd also given me a magical cornucopia in case I ever needed her again. I was going to miss seeing her for Sunday breakfast.

Chris's phone beeped for attention. He glanced at the screen and scowled. "It's my agent. She said she's about to call me. I'm going to tell her we'll be in the air soon and I'll lose my signal."

"I don't think that happens anymore," I said. "Technology's come a long way since your last flip phone."

"Let's pretend technology is old and slow so I can have a few hours of peace," Chris said, then his phone rang. He brought it to his ear and closed his eyes. "Hi, Maisie. Yes, we're about to board." Chris got up and walked to the end of the aisle, his shoulders slumping as he listened to whatever his agent was saying.

"I thought his publisher was pleased with the draft he sent over," Robert said. A few feet away, Chris pinched the bridge of his nose.

"From what Chris said, they loved it." That the publisher was pleased with Chris's latest novel wasn't a surprise. He was a brilliant writer, and I wasn't just saying that because he's my big brother. His last book had sold an amazing amount of copies, and had been translated into a dozen languages. There was even talk of a movie deal. If that isn't objective evidence of his skill, I don't know what is.

"Perhaps we should reschedule our flight and allow time for Christopher to sort out his business here," Robert suggested.

"Maybe you should have hitched a ride with Anya," I said. "Then you could avoid the big, scary airplane."

Robert scowled. "I should have arranged for our passage on a ship regardless o' your desire to soar wi' the birds." He leaned closer, and added, "Ye are certain this mode o' transport will no' harm the bairn?"

"Of course it won't," I said with more confidence than I felt. Both my doctor and about a thousand internet searches on my part had assured me that there was nothing wrong with a woman traveling by air in her first trimester of pregnancy, provided that the pregnancy in question wasn't high risk. Mine wasn't, and while I didn't mind allaying Robert's fears whenever I could, I did not think spending six days cooped up on a boat would be good for any of us.

I grasped his hand and squeezed. "We'll be okay. Honest." When Robert squeezed back, I knew he believed me. Chris ended his call and returned to his seat.

"Fun talk with Maisie?" I asked.

"Contract talk with Maisie," he replied. "So no, not fun, but necessary. I'm glad she's handling the bulk of it."

"At least you have other things to think about," I said. "Are you excited to meet Anya's family?"

"Ah, no. Terrified is more like it," Chris replied. "And I sort of met her mother when I was at the pub with Sorcha." He tilted back his head and looked at the ceiling. "If there is a God, making Beira forget all of that would make me a devoted follower for the rest of my days."

Robert laughed and clapped Chris on the shoulder. "That is no' how He works. Ye must learn from your mistakes, lad, no' sweep them under the rug like so much dust."

Chris frowned. "Based on the amount of mistakes I've made, if I learned something from every one of them, I would qualify for a second doctorate."

A voice came over the loudspeaker announcing our flight. As we queued up to board the plane, Robert took my carryon bag from me and slung it over his shoulder. Ever since he'd known about the baby, he'd been the most loving, overprotective man on earth, and I was enjoying every minute of it.

"All right," I said, clutching my boarding pass. "Let's go start a new life."

THE CARETAKER

D espite Robert's apprehensions, we had an uneventful flight across the Atlantic and landed in Edinburgh early the next morning. I'd even managed to sleep on the plane, which was a first for me. Robert claimed he'd slept as well, though Chris hadn't gotten any rest. Apparently, his agent kept texting him bits of contract jargon for him to review. So much for his "no Wi-Fi in the air" excuse.

When Chris's agent wasn't annoying the living crap out of him with legal terms, the flight attendants took turns flirting with him. That wasn't surprising, since between the two of us he'd always been the better looking sibling. He was the spitting image of our Scandinavian mother, from his blond hair to his Nordic blue eyes. Chris had always worn his hair longer on top, and the shock of pale hair coupled with his perpetually tan skin made him look more like a surfer than someone who wrote mysteries set in Elizabethan England.

As for me, I'd inherited my pale, freckly skin and brown hair from our father, along with a host of other questionable traits. It was as if Mom had passed all of her good DNA on to Chris, and by the time I'd come along, she didn't have anything left to give me, save for my blue eyes. That blue shade was the only physical feature Chris and I shared.

Now Robert's looks were an altogether different story. He was handsome in a hero from a paperback romance sort of way, with his dark, wavy hair, pale blue eyes, and a smile that, even after seeing it hundreds of times, still made me forget my name. The flight attendants had tried flirting with him too, but Robert had immediately grabbed my hand and called me his bride, and went on about how we were moving back home to Scotland, and expecting a baby in a few months. Robert wasn't just handsome, he was steadfast. I loved that about him.

After the plane landed, and we completed such unexciting tasks as disembarking, getting our luggage sorted out, and renting a car, the three of us were on the road and heading toward our cottage in Crail. I ended up driving the rental, which was something Chris wouldn't stop complaining about.

"It's so cramped back here it's like a second glove box," he whined from the back seat.

"Robert can't sit back there," I said. Again. "He's way too tall. I can't sit there, because get car sick in the back. Besides, when your car gets here, you can drive it all over the place."

"I still can no' believe ye spent all that money to ship that vehicle o'erseas," Robert said. "Could ye no' ha' sold it in New York and used the funds to purchase another? I'm sure they sell cars here in Scotland."

"Chris loves his car." I smirked at him in the rearview mirror. "It's a three. Chris, tell Robert about the special three."

"It's a BMW 325i," Chris huffed. "The three signifies the series. Why are you driving, again?"

"Because you don't want me puking on you," I replied. "Anyway, Chris's car has custom everything. He saved for years to get it exactly how he wanted it."

"The cost of shipping is also less than ten percent of what it's worth," Chris added. "You can't just stroll into a dealership and buy a car like mine."

"'Tis a certainly lovely machine," Robert said, and resumed watching the countryside speed by through the side window. I imagined that any sentimental feelings Robert had had toward possessions had dissolved during his time as Nicnevin's prisoner and assassin, when he'd owned nothing but his sword, shield, and the clothes on his back. Chris, however, still had a thing for worldly goods.

I turned down the scrabbly road that led to the cottage, and felt a sense of peace I'd never experienced in New York. Even though we hadn't been away from Crail for all that long, I'd missed the quaint little house with its walled garden. Before I'd come to Scotland, I'd thought I had my entire life planned out; I was on track to earn my doctorate in geology, after which I'd spend the next decade or so teaching and doing fieldwork, and then move fully into research. All of that changed when I freed Robert from the Seelie Queen's curse.

After a few more run-ins with the supernatural side of things, the Seelie King figured out that I'm a walker. That means I have the ability to pass from one dimension to another—such as from here to fairyland—with ease. It wasn't as fun as Anya's ability to teleport, but my talent has come in handy more than once.

As we approached the cottage, I noticed a very large, very shiny black truck parked near the front door. It wasn't one of the beat-up old farm trucks which were common in and around the village. This truck wasn't for work so much as it was a status symbol. I wondered who—or what—thought we were worthy of such a display.

"Whose truck is that?" I asked. "Chris, does Anya drive?"

"I don't think so." He leaned forward and peered at the truck. "Even if she did, I don't think she'd be driving that."

"It most likely belongs to a neighbor checking up on the place," Robert said. "When I kept a home in Aberfoyle, me neighbors were in and out all day."

I refrained from mentioning that we didn't know anyone except fairies in Crail, and that even if we had known a few humans, no one knew we were coming back. "Okay, let's hope it's owned by a friendly villager and not an axe murderer." I parked the car and faced Robert. "You go first."

Robert laughed as he exited the rental, but I was serious. Sending the man with the sword into the unknown situation first was my and Chris's best chance at survival. Robert strode up to the front door and entered without knocking—it was our house, after all—and stopped dead right inside the doorway.

"What is it?" I asked.

"Hello there," came a man's voice from inside the cottage. Robert stepped aside, and I saw Dougal MacKay, the man Chris and I had dealt with when we'd originally rented the place eight months ago. He'd handed us two sets of keys and a map, and we hadn't seen him since. "I was hopin' to catch the lot o' ye this mornin'. How was your flight?"

"Good, it was good," I replied, too stunned to be anything other than polite. "Mr. MacKay, please don't take this the wrong way, but we weren't expecting to see you."

"I expect ye weren't," he said. "After the two o' ye became the owners o' this fine piece o' property, I stayed on as caretaker, keeping up the structure and doin' a few odd jobs here and there."

"Ye always were one for odd jobs," Robert said.

I blinked, at first assuming I'd misheard. The way Robert was glaring at Dougal told me I'd heard things just fine.

"You two know each other?" I asked. Robert had been with us when we arrived at the cottage back in September, but he had stayed outside while Chris and I had signed all of the assorted rental forms, therefore he hadn't seen Dougal.

"Aye, that we do," Robert replied. "Don't we, Dougal?"

Dougal nodded. "'Tis the truth."

"Great, we're all friends here," Chris said as he dropped his suitcase in front of his bedroom door. "Mr. MacKay, has a blonde woman named Anya come by?"

"She most certainly has, but she kept mostly to the garden, visitin' with the wights," Dougal replied. "She left some time ago. I expect she's passing time at the pub with her mum, and I do hear a cold one callin' me name. Welcome back to Crail. I shall look in on ye in a day or so."

Dougal tipped his hat and exited the cottage, shutting the door behind him. Once he was gone, I faced Robert. "How exactly do you know him?" I demanded, feeling the first waves of panic welling up inside me. If Dougal knew about the wights and Anya's mother, that meant he was someone or something from fairy and who knows why he was really in our house. Robert took one look at me wringing my hands, and guided me toward the kitchen table.

"Get off your feet," he said, and I sat on one of the wooden chairs. "I am well acquainted with Dougal, and have been since before I was taken to Elphame."

"Oh." We hadn't been in Scotland for twelve hours yet, and the supernatural world was already messing with us. "I don't suppose he's one of the good guys?"

Robert snorted. "He moves between the Seelie and Unseelie courts as it suits him. Sometimes both sides want his head on a pike, but as o' yet the old phooka has outsmarted them all."

"Phooka," Chris said. "So he's a fairy?"

"Aye," Robert replied. "And a fairy spy, at that."

"Our caretaker is spying on us," Chris said. "Great."

"We don't know that," I said. "We should keep an eye on him, but let's not jump to conclusions."

"Oh, I will keep both me eyes on him," Robert said. "I suppose the current question is, how is he affiliated with this cottage?"

"I don't know," I replied. "Before, when we rented this place, it was through the Spiritual Sights tour." I leaned back and stared at the ceiling. "The tour that was set up by Nicnevin. I guess that explains how Fionnlagh was able to give us this place."

Robert grunted. "Then perhaps MacKay is still working with the Seelie."

"Is that good?" I asked.

"It's certainly better than the alternative."

"Okay, well, I hope you two don't mind if I table this crisis for now," Chris said. "I'm going to go find my girlfriend."

I tossed Chris the rental's keys. "Tell Beira we said hi."

"Will do."

Chris grabbed his jacket and left in search of Anya. I looked around the cottage, and noted that everything was exactly the same as we'd left it. The African violet Robert had given me was still on the windowsill above the kitchen sink; as I watched, a lavender wight delivered it a handful of water. The furniture didn't even look dusty, which made me wonder if Dougal had spent the day cleaning the place up. Or if some kind of housecleaning spell was keeping things tidy.

Crap. I really hoped that Dougal had been wielding a mop and a dust cloth, and not any sort of questionable magic inside our house.

"Wyatt?" I called. A moment later, the tiny, bright blue fairy flew in through the kitchen window and landed on the table in front of me.

"Hello, Mistress Stewart." Wyatt turned toward Robert and bowed. "Master Kirk. How was your journey?"

"It was good. I'm glad you guys took care of my violet," I added, and Wyatt beamed. "What do you know about the caretaker, Dougal?"

"Very little, I'm afraid," he replied. "He started coming to the cottage while I was across the water with you, mistress. The others say that he stops by once or twice a week."

"What does he do when he's here?" Robert asked.

"He sweeps, mostly. Homes are much dirtier than gardens."

I smiled. "That's because homes don't have wights to take care of them. Has he ever worked any magic here?"

"Not to my knowledge, mistress."

"Thank you, Wyatt. I appreciate what you've told me."

Wyatt nodded, then he flew back to the garden. I watched him until he disappeared beyond the window frame.

"Tell me what's goin' through that head o' yours," Robert prompted-ed.

"Lots of stuff," I replied. "What should we do about Dougal? And should we move out of the cottage?"

Robert frowned a bit, and rubbed the back of his neck. "As for what's to be done about MacKay, I say we watch and wait for now. Best to know his game afore we make a move, and accidentally play into his hands."

"You really think he's planning something?"

Robert snorted. "That one is always scheming." He leaned forward and took my hands in his. "As for the cottage, it was fair given to us by the Seelie King. I would no' wish to incur his ire if we were to abandon such a fine gift."

"Good point." The last thing we needed was more pissed off gods in our lives. Supposedly, the *geas* Hades had placed on Demeter would keep her from harassing us for the next eight years, but if anyone could find a loophole in that spell, it was my former mentor.

Speaking of Demeter, in the front pocket of my hooded sweatshirt I carried one of my most prized possessions: the cornucopia that Persephone had given me. It was a miniature version of the cornucopia that had pride of place in the back room of her restaurant in Queens, and she'd promised that if I ever needed anything I just needed to ask. She hadn't said if I should ask the cornucopia directly or just shout her name into the air, but I was betting on the former.

I walked across the cottage's living area and set the cornucopia on the long shelf above the electric fireplace. "Think it looks good there?"

"I do," Robert replied. "Makes this house a bit more o' a home."

"Now what should we do now?" I asked, dreading all the unpacking in our future.

Robert stood beside me and straightened the cornucopia. "I believe we should first visit our bedchamber," he began, a slow smile spreading across his face, "and ensure that all is as we left it."

"Oh? And will this be a thorough inspection?"

"Aye. Quite thorough." He wrapped an arm around me, and traced my cheek with his other hand. "And afterward, we can decide where we'd like to set up the cradle."

I laughed and hid my face against his chest. "I can't believe we're going to have a baby."

He kissed my hair. "Good things happen to good people." We held each other for a moment, then he continued, "Perhaps I can secure myself an axe and fell some trees. I'd like to start building it sooner rather than later."

I drew back and looked up at him. "You're going to *build* a cradle?"

"O' course I am. She'll need a place to sleep."

I sighed and rested my cheek against his chest. "They have stores where you can buy lumber. Already cut, seasoned, what have you. Most of them even deliver, so we won't have to worry about hauling the supplies back home. Or we could just buy an already made cradle."

"Bah. What kind o' man would let his babe rest in something store bought? A man o' weak morals, I say."

"You are the most old-fashioned man in the world, you know that?"

"Aye. That's why ye love me so."

AN UNHAPPY REUNION

I drove from the cottage straight to the center of Crail and left the rental car in the lot near the Mercat Cross; it was Rina's favorite spot the village, since the column was topped with a statue of a Scotland's national animal, a unicorn. It was the same lot where I used to park the last rental car I'd had in Scotland, all those months ago when I'd go into town to be with Nicnevin, though she'd been calling herself Sorcha at the time. And now I was back, eagerly anticipating spending time with another fairy woman I was head over heels in love with. The difference was that this time, I was in love with Anya, and she loved me back.

I took a deep breath and consciously set all thoughts of Nicnevin aside. I had no desire to see the Seelie Queen ever again, but Anya's mother was Beira, the Cailleach Bheur of myth and legend. For all I knew, Beira could read minds just as easily as she could whip up some frost on a pumpkin, and I did not need a stray thought about Nicnevin sullying our first formal meeting.

Crail's streets were almost empty, and a few minutes after I exited the car, I was opening the pub's door. The interior was just the same as it had been when I used to come here with Sorcha; dim lighting, highly polished woodwork, and plush leather booths. The first time

I'd entered the pub, I'd been lamenting the end of my relationship with my fiancée, Olivia. The irony of me being at that same pub in order to meet Anya's mother was not lost on me.

My gaze found Anya almost immediately. She was sitting on a stool at the far end of the bar, her hands folded neatly in her lap and her spine straight as an arrow. Her yellow hair was golden in the low light, and her pale skin shone. My God, she was beautiful.

Anya noticed me and smiled. I waved and started toward her, but she shook her head slightly. When I raised my brows, she nodded toward the bar and I saw her mother filling pint glasses and chatting with her customers. Why Beira worked as a barmaid was a mystery, but one I could solve at another time. Beira's hair was long and yellow like Anya's, but she had garlands of tiny pink and blue flowers woven into the length of it. Her eyes flashed cold and hard, and when Beira laughed, I saw rows and rows of tiny teeth that glinted like diamonds. I was suddenly glad that Anya did not take after her mother with regard to her dental attributes.

Another feature of Anya's that differed from her mother was her eyes. Beira's eyes were much like human eyes, a bright and piercing blue, but otherwise unremarkable. Anya's eyes were something else entirely. They were an iridescent gray, somewhere between the gift of a rainbow on a dreary day and an oil slick floating atop a pond, and since she didn't have pupils or irises that gray sheen stretched from her upper to lower lashes. Her eyes also didn't reflect their surroundings, which made me feel as if they really were gateways to her soul. I was confident that Anya had the most beautiful eyes in the world.

As you've probably guessed by now, I can see through fae glamours. I've had that ability ever since Nicnevin led me into her bed, and then to Elphame. That meant I saw Anya and her mother's true forms, not whatever guise they were wearing to blend in with the mortals. The rest of the pub's patrons saw a young, athletic blonde woman sitting at the bar, while a slightly older blonde woman served drinks, not the Winter Queen and her daughter. Even though I'd gained this sight through rather harrowing means, I was glad to see the truth of things.

Based on Anya's clues, I guessed that I was supposed to greet her mother first. That made sense, since Beira was fairy royalty. Being that it was late March, I wondered if that meant Beira's strength—however that may manifest—was waning. I also wondered if her appearance became more mortal in the warmer months, if such a thing was possible. And why would the Queen of Winter wear spring flowers in her hair?

I approached the bar and claimed the stool on Anya's left, and waited for Beira to notice me. I didn't have to wait long.

"And here he is," Beira announced when she caught sight of me. "The fool who thinks he is worthy o' me only daughter."

My mouth went dry as my palms started to sweat. I hadn't expected insta-love from Beira, but neither had I expected instant hatred. "Hello, ah." I leaned toward Anya, and whispered, "What should I call her?"

"Ye do no' need to call me anythin'," Beira roared. "Get on with ye, go back to warmin' Nicnevin's bed, and leave us be. We've had enough o' the likes o' ye."

"That wasn't my fault," I said. "Nicnevin put a spell on me!"

"You and yours have been causing me problems for years, long afore ye crossed the Seelie Queen's path," Beira said. "Your family is a blight upon this island, from your ancestors all the way down to your fool sister."

Queen of Winter or no, no one talked about Rina that way. "What is your problem with my sister?" I demanded.

Anya gasped, but a glare from Beira silenced her. "When Karina loosed the gallowglass from the Minister's Pine, she loosed a few other beasties as well. If she's a speck of morals, she'll hie herself back to Doon Hill and see to her messes."

"I'll tell her," I said, even though I had no idea what beasties she was talking about. Hopefully Rina and Robert could figure out who or what had upset Beira. "What else has my family supposedly done to yours?"

Beira cocked an eyebrow. "Are ye attempting to make amends for your ancestor's misdeeds?"

"If a wrong has been done and I can fix it, I will," I said.

Beira nodded. "Perhaps your mother's blood is a good influence over your father's. 'Twas his line that caused us so much hurt, ye ken."

I swallowed hard, and ignored the lump in my throat. I was in no position to defend my deceased parents against a pissed off fairy. "Well? Tell me about it. What have the Stewarts done to you?"

"Oh, 'twas long afore ye went by that name," Beira replied. "And 'twas in many, many ways. I'll begin with the worst offense, for if ye can right that, then ye surely are a man apart from that cur. The one who wronged us fancied himself an alchemist, worked for the king, even. But he was a liar, and men who are liars destroy all they touch."

I couldn't argue with that. "Go on."

"He wanted fame, and set about hunting giants. For all that he called himself a wizard, the old fart knew little o' his craft, and more often than no' his spells misfired. But then he went after a friend o' mine, one o' the closest friends I have e're had, and he turned her to stone."

Beira slammed a full pint glass down on the bar, startling me. I hadn't even seen her pour it. "Drink your ale, then go reverse what he's done. I do no' want to see hide nor hair o' ye until then."

With that Beira spun around and stalked through the swinging doors and the end of the bar, and disappeared into a back room. I turned toward Anya, to ask her who this friend was and where I could find the stone, but her stool was empty.

She'd left. She hadn't said a single word to me.

I sat at the bar for more than an hour, waiting for Beira to come out from the back room or Anya to return from wherever she gone. During that time I finished my beer and signaled for a second. When I asked the replacement bartender where Beira had gone, he had no idea what I was talking about.

"I've been the only one working all day," he replied.

"Is there a waitress, then?" I pressed. "Blonde, loud woman?"

"No and no," he replied. "I'll keep an eye out for loud blondes, though. Can't have too many o' them hangin' about."

The bartender laughed and left me to my confusion. I finished the second beer, then I left the pub and walked back toward the rental car. I was halfway there before I decided what my next move should be.

Beira was angry with me because someone had turned one of her friends to stone. Whether or not the man who was responsible for that act was related to me wasn't the point. The point was that Beira wanted me to prove myself worthy of Anya. More than anything, I wanted to prove that, too.

Since this test involved me freeing a woman from a stone, I needed to brush up on the local folklore and find out if any of these mountains or rings of boulders had a similar legend attached to them. There could only be what, ten thousand such monuments in the UK, if not Scotland alone? I could have picked Rob's brain for clues—he did have the market cornered on local legends—but I wanted to figure this out on my own. Beira had tasked me, not the gallowglass, with helping her friend. Luckily, I knew someone who worked right next to one of the greatest libraries in the world.

I pulled out my phone and called Ethan Jacobsen, an old friend of mine who taught at the nearby university, St. Andrews. I ended up leaving him a message, but that was fine. He'd always been good about returning calls. My next call was to the cottage.

A NEW COURT

An endless chiming noise woke me. My eyes blinked open, and for a moment I couldn't remember where I was... Then I remembered the mad Olympians, all the boxes we'd packed and stacked as Robert and I had cleared out my apartment, and the long flight across the ocean. The baby growing inside me. I was with Robert at our cottage in Scotland, and that chiming was my phone clamoring for attention.

I rolled over and saw him lying beside me, fully dressed as I was. We'd gone into the bedroom as planned, and had promptly fallen asleep.

"Hey." I nudged Robert until his eyes opened. "I guess the jet lag caught up with us."

Robert's brow quirked in the way it always did when I used a modern term he didn't understand. I'd always liked that. "That, or our bairn wore ye out yet again," he said. He moved to kiss me, then the chimes started up again.

"I have got to change that ringtone," I muttered as I sat up.

"I shall answer the caller," Robert announced, and he got out of bed and went in search of my phone. I flopped back down on the bed and burrowed under the covers. I was wide awake, thanks to the incessant ringing, but the down comforter was hard to resist. Robert returned a few minutes later, and the look on his face told me that snuggle time was over.

"That was Christopher," he began, then he told me how Beira was mad at him because of something an ancestor of ours had done a few centuries ago. She was also mad about something I'd done, but that stemmed from a more recent event: freeing Robert from the Minister's Pine on Doon Hill.

"Do you think one of my ancestors really did something to one of Beira's friends?" I asked Robert when he was done relaying Chris's words.

"'Tis a possibility," he replied. "In my time, I've seen all manner of creatures harmed by magic as a result o' anger or even out of spite. When magic ran thick among the trees strange and unusual punishments were a common enough occurrence."

I shivered. "Maybe us mortals really are better off without magic."

"Karina, there is also the matter of Beira accusin' ye of setting creatures and such free from Elphame."

"How is that even possible?" I asked. "It's like she's blaming me for creating a portal. Back then I had no idea how to do that. I hadn't even known I was a walker."

"But ye did open a portal when ye freed me," Robert pointed out.

"Crap." If opening a portal was really as easy as saying a few words to a tree—which was all I'd done to the Minister's Pine—I may have left a ton of portals open all over New York. "Do you think we, um, left the door open?"

"I do no' ken, but we can find out easily enough." Robert stood and offered me a hand. "My love, I believe it is time we returned to Doon Hill."

I yawned and stretched. "What time is it?"

"A quarter to three."

"All right, let's go and get this over with." I left our bedroom and walked toward the kitchen counter, and saw the empty key peg. "Dammit, Chris took the rental car."

Robert glanced out the front window. "MacKay left his truck behind. Perhaps we're meant to borrow it?"

"I thought you said he was one of the bad guys." Despite saying that, I opened the front door and approached the truck. It was awfully shiny, and the keys were sitting in plain view right on the dashboard. "He left the keys behind, too."

Robert opened the driver's door and gestured for me to enter. "Well, then. In light of this most serendipitous turn, I think it is best we take the truck. After all, we do want to know what Beira is so worked up about. Shall we?"

I gave Robert some side eye, then hopped inside the truck, marveling at the posh upholstery and state-of-the-art-dashboard. Dougal's truck was much nicer than our rental car. After Robert sat in the passenger seat, I turned the key and the engine purred to life. Nice.

"Best buckle up," Robert said as he fastened his seatbelt.

"Safety first," I said as I did the same. "I hope we don't end up regretting this. The truck, Doon Hill, any of it."

"Me as well," Robert said.

We drove from Crail to Aberfoyle straight through, without stopping once. Traffic had been on our side, and it took us just under ninety minutes to complete the trip. I parked in the lot in the center of the village, then Robert and I got out and looked toward the bridge that spanned the River Forth.

"Here we are," I said. "Right where it all began."

"Aye." Robert took my hand, and we started across the bridge. Beyond that, the trail took us past the kirk where Robert had presided over his parishioners back in the seventeenth century. The kirk itself was in ruins, but the adjacent graveyard was in good condition, if a bit overgrown.

"Want to visit the churchyard?" I asked.

Robert shook his head. "Not in the least. The thought o' seein' me own grave gives me the chills, no matter that 'tis an empty grave."

"I hadn't thought of that," I mumbled. I stooped and picked up a stone that had caught my eye. The body of the stone was salmon pink, and it was decorated with regularly spaced flecks of gray. I bet it would look fantastic after a trip through the rock tumbler.

"What's that?" Robert asked.

"Just some granite." I straightened and shoved the stone in my pocket. "Remember back when I was just a geologist?"

Robert draped his arm around my shoulders and laughed. "Karina, ye have ne'er been 'just' anything."

"After we settle in, maybe we can go prospecting," I said. "We can get some fun stones, and maybe find some fossils."

"And ye can work on your final paper for your doctorate," Robert added.

"Yeah. That too."

We walked on, past the kirk and graveyard, and followed the trail up to Doon Hill. The trail was a bit muddy thanks to the early spring rains, but we managed. Well, I managed; Robert hiked up the hill like an Olympic athlete. As the trail sloped upward, the forest was exactly as I remembered it, but soon the landscape became crowded with some rather unusual decorations.

"Is that supposed to be one of the Good People?" I asked. Robert turned around, his mouth curled up as if to laugh at a joke, then he saw what I was looking at. On the ground situated next to the trail was a little porcelain figure of a girl. She had brown hair, wore a lavender dress, and attached to her back were glittery pink wings.

"I suppose it is." Robert crouched down to get a better look at it. "Look, there are a few more hidden among the moss."

"Huh." I saw three more figurines set just off the trail, and even more scattered along the path as far as I could see them. All together, there were at least two dozen of the tiny statues set up like a fairy diorama. "Has someone been decorating the trail?"

"Perhaps they are offerings," Robert said as he stood.

"Offerings to what?" I wondered. "I thought the Good People liked bowls of milk and fresh bread."

Robert didn't answer, but his furrowed brow spoke volumes. "Let's keep moving," he said. "Stay close to me."

"Staying."

We continued on up the hill, and the offerings grew in both number and strangeness. The little fairy figurines gave way to bigger and more elaborate items, such as jewelry draped from tree branches and minia-ture wooden houses, many of which were carved right into living tree trunks. I hoped no one, fairy or otherwise, was keeping watch from those tiny windows.

"Do you think the local tourist board is decorating the hill, and trying to get more vacationers to come out here?" I asked. "Maybe this is all part of a plan to increase spending in town."

"That is a good assumption," Robert said. We reached the top of the hill and the entrance to the clearing. Robert and I took another step forward, then he extended his arm, barring me from going any further up the trail.

"What's wrong?" I asked.

"I believe this hill is plagued with tourists of a different sort."

He nodded toward the Minister's Pine. When I saw what he saw, I clapped my hands over my mouth to keep from screaming.

Standing not fifty feet up the trail were Good People, fairies, whatever you wanted to call them, and the clearing was packed with more types of creatures than I had names for. There were beautiful ones straight out of a seventies fantasy movie standing right next to the ugliest creatures I'd ever seen, and everything in between. Some were human sized, some were tinier than the wights, and some of them seemed to be made of rocks and plants instead of flesh and blood. Worst of all, in the center of the clearing was a crude wooden chair set on a lopsided platform. These fairies had built a throne.

"They've created a court," Robert whispered. "No' Seelie nor Unseelie, as far as I can tell. This is something altogether different, akin to the Wild Fae of old."

"Who exactly are the Wild Fae?"

"Those no' beholden to either court."

That could not be good. "How is the clearing so big?" When I'd stood in this clearing last summer, it had been a good size, but it could only hold thirty, maybe fifty people if you really packed them in. Now the packed earth that surrounded the Minister's Pine stretched back the length of a football field. "Did they clear cut the forest?"

"I think what we are seeing is a bit of Elphame leaking into our world. It seems that Beira was right in that when ye brought me through the door in the pine, we left it open a smidge."

Crap.

This was what Beira had meant about me cleaning up my messes. It was why she was mad at Chris, too, and why she thought Anya and all of Scotland would be better off without both of us living here. We were making a mess of her home. The evidence was plain before me.

As I gazed out across this new court, I saw a familiar face. "Uncle John?"

Robert faced me. "What did ye say? Uncle?"

"Yeah." I nodded toward the far left side of the Ministers Pine. "See that tall, thin man wearing the blue sweater, khakis, and glasses? He looks just like my Uncle John. My dad's uncle, really. I haven't seen him in years."

Robert put his hand on my elbow and drew me down the trail and away from the gathering. "Could this uncle be the relation o' yours Beira mentioned to Christopher?"

"I don't see how," I replied. "The last I heard, he was trying to become a professional poker player. In fact, he'd always been a gambler. I remember my parents talking about it."

Robert gazed toward the gathering. "How old was this uncle when ye were a wee lass?"

"Not much older than my dad," I replied. "Forties, maybe fifty? I don't remember him having gray hair, or anything like that." I frowned. "Now that I think about it, I don't know how he was related to us. My dad's father only had two sisters, and his mother was an only child."

Robert grunted. "Follow me."

We moved in a circular path through the trees along the edge of the clearing until we were close to where the man who resembled Uncle John was standing.

"Karina, how old does that man appear to be?"

I stared at him for a few moments before I replied. "If that's my uncle, he hasn't aged a day in fifteen years."

"If that's your uncle, I'd like to find out how he's associated with the Good People and this new court," Robert said.

"What should we do?" I asked. "Go over and say hi?"

Robert shook his head. "I will no' risk ye among all those creatures," he said, then he looked at the sky. "'Twill be night soon, which means we should be getting home. We shall be patient, and wait for a better time to deal with this."

I blew out a breath and leaned against Robert. "I hate waiting."

"I ken that." He patted my midsection, and added, "Best get used to it, at least for the next few months."

STORIES TO TELL

I didn't wait for Ethan to return my call before I headed over to St. Andrews. The university town was less than an hour's drive from Crail, and I wanted to get started on my research into local giant folklore as soon as possible. Granted, the best person to ask about one of Beira's friends getting turned into stone was Rob; he had been an expert in local lore long before he'd been captured by the Seelie Queen and earned the title of gallowglass.

Even though Rob was undoubtedly the best man for the job, I wanted to leave him and Rina out of my latest mess, at least for now. They were so excited about the baby, and I didn't want to do anything to dampen that. Besides, at some point I needed to figure out how to handle my love life without my sister's help, if you could even call what Anya and I shared any semblance of love.

If she loved me, wouldn't she be here with me, helping me figure this out? Or at least tell me where she'd gone? Since Anya and I had met in New York, I had no idea of where she'd go in Scotland, or who she'd confide in, and I didn't know where to look for her. Hell, I barely remembered Beira from my last trip to Crail, even though Sorcha and I had spent a lot of time in that pub. What I did remember was how

Sorcha's eyes had glinted in the light, the way her dark hair tumbled over her shoulders and grazed the top of her breasts...

I shook my head, but the images of Sorcha remained. Why couldn't I stop picturing her? I hadn't thought about Sorcha in months, but now everything I saw reminded me of her. Specifically, of her naked. Maybe returning to Scotland had unearthed some old memories, or maybe these past days I'd spent without Anya had left me more frustrated than I'd realized. Whatever the cause, it needed to stop.

As I drove toward St. Andrews, a terrible thought coalesced in the forefront of my mind: maybe I was fixating on my time with Sorcha because Anya and I just weren't meant to be together.

"Screw that," I muttered to the steering wheel. "I'm sick of fate or karma or whatever telling me who I can and can't love. It doesn't matter if Beira likes me. All that matters is that Anya likes me."

My motivational speech lifted my spirits, and it wasn't long before I parked the car and was striding down the town's cobbled streets. I was halfway to the campus when my phone buzzed. It was Ethan.

"Ethan," I greeted. "You'll never guess where I am, and man, do I have stories to tell you."

Ethan and I had something of a history together. We'd known each other since middle school, though we'd never hung out until the eleventh grade. That was the year both of our girlfriends dumped us on Valentine's Day and we'd ended up hooking up with each other at the school dance.

We hadn't worked out as a couple, and were back to friend status within a few weeks. Good friends, actually; we'd both studied English at Carson University in New York, and had ended up earning our doctorates on the same day. Our joint graduation party was the second time we'd hooked up, and the second time we'd ended up staying friends. Ethan's friendship was one of the few constants in my life, and I loved him almost as much as I loved Rina. I suppose it was only natural I went to him for help about Anya.

Ethan met me in St. Andrews outside the British Golf Museum—possibly the most Scottish place in all of Scotland—and we went to a local pub to catch up. After he'd regaled me with tales of rowdy students and stellar essay submissions, I dropped the bigger of my two bombshells on him.

"You remember my sister?" I asked.

"Sweet little Rina," Ethan said. "How could I ever forget that angel? If it wasn't for her, I would have failed algebra. And chemistry."

I laughed; if Rob heard Ethan refer to Rina like that, I'd probably be down a friend. "That angel's all grown up, and get this? She's having a baby!"

"What? When? With who?"

"Not for a while yet," I replied. "Baby's due at the end of summer. As for the father, she met him here in Scotland during our trip last summer. Robert Kirk's his name."

Ethan grunted. "Same name as a fellow who wrote a book about fairies a few centuries back."

I raised an eyebrow as I raised my pint glass. "That's him," I said, then I drank.

Ethan guffawed. "Right, and I'm the Easter Bunny. So tell me about this new woman in your life. Anya, is it?"

"Yeah. Anya." I set down my glass and took a deep breath. "Her mother's the head of her family. Very matriarchal. She, ah, happens to hate me."

"The legendary Stewart charm hasn't won her over?"

"The Stewart charm seems to be the problem. She started going on about how my family's caused hers nothing but problems." I drank more beer; thinking about Beira made me unusually thirsty. "Problems reaching back years. Centuries, even."

"Is that true?" Ethan asked.

"I don't see how it could be," I replied. "My father was Scottish, but his family immigrated to America over two hundred years ago. What could have happened that long ago that's upsetting her today?"

Ethan leaned back and drained his pint glass. "Scots have long memories, and they'll hold a grudge so tightly they'll pass it from one generation to the next. You may as well accept that you've somehow wronged her, and try to get back in her good graces a different way. Any idea what she likes, aside from breaking your balls?"

"She does like folklore. Any idea where I can pick up a few books, so I could brush up on the local legends?"

"You sure that's something she'd appreciate?"

"Oh, yeah. She'd appreciate that a great deal."

THE CAILLEACH BHEUR
LEAVES HER MARK

The next morning started out overcast, which wasn't unusual for early spring in Scotland. What was unusual was my wardrobe conspiring against me.

"This is not working," I muttered to myself.

"What's that, now?" Robert called from the kitchen.

"My jeans. They fit yesterday, but now they, um, shrunk."

I was standing in front of the full-length mirror in our bedroom, fully clothed save for my unbuttoned jeans. I turned from side to side as I studied my reflection, observing how they still fit my legs and hips, but not my waist.

Robert poked his head into the room and smiled. "Shrunk, eh? More like you grew. Best wear those stretchy pants o' yours."

I glared at him, and resumed trying to suck in my stomach. No luck. Evidently pregnant bellies understood the concept of out, but not in. "This is all your fault."

Robert laughed at that, and returned to whatever he'd been doing in the kitchen. I took off my most traitorous piece of clothing and stowed it in a dresser drawer. After pulling on my stupid stretchy pants, I went out to the kitchen to see what Robert was up to.

"What's all this?" I asked when I saw the food spread across the table.

"Breakfast is what it is," he replied. "I went out while ye were still asleep."

"Oh." I'd wondered why I'd woken up alone. "This looks great. Thank you."

"Ye can thank me by eatin', love," he said, and he didn't have to tell me twice. Robert had brought home egg and cheese filled rolls, tattie scones, and an assortment of muffins and other sweet treats. We had coffee, too, courtesy of our pre-programmable coffee maker.

"Wait," I said, looking over the food. "Where's the bacon?"

"I ate it on the way home," Robert replied. "I did no' wish to offend ye with the meat stink, as ye refer to it."

I smiled and grabbed a tattie scone. "Did Chris even come home last night?"

"Neither he nor Anya returned," Robert replied. "What do ye think they got up to?" Before I could speculate on what adventures my brother and his fairy girlfriend may have had, Chris walked through the front door.

"Morning," I said. When no one entered behind him, I asked, "Is Anya with you?"

"I don't know where she is. I was with Ethan, at St. Andrews." Chris sat at the table and looked over the food. "I see breakfast happened."

"It has," I said.

"Help yourself," Robert added.

Chris started making himself a plate while I stared at Robert. He shrugged, which I took to mean that he had no idea what might have happened between Chris and Anya, or Chris and Ethan, for that matter.

Chris frowned after he'd rifled through the assorted boxes. "Where's the bacon, sausage... There isn't even any haggis. What kind of Scottish breakfast is this?" Chris looked from me to Robert. Robert tipped his head toward me and shrugged.

"Seriously, Rina?," Chris asked. "None of us can have meat?"

"You can have all the meat you want, as long as I don't have to smell it."

"How much longer are you going to be pregnant, anyway?" Chris asked.

"Fifty years. How's Ethan?"

"Good. He's helping me research some local folklore."

Robert and I shared a glance. "What kind of local folklore?" I asked.

"Giants trapped in stone." Chris resumed eating, and I resisted the urge to kick him under the table. Barely.

"And why are we researching stone giants?" I asked.

The front door opened, and Anya stepped inside. "Because of me. Me mum, actually," she said.

"Hi, Anya," I said. "Are you hungry? Robert brought home enough food to feed an army."

"No, thank you," she replied. "Christopher, did you tell them?"

"I was about to." Chris didn't look at Anya as he spoke. "As I told Rob yesterday on the phone, Beira's mad because of something an ancestor of ours did. Specifically, one of her friends got trapped in stone, and she claims said ancestor is responsible."

"Really?" I asked, while Robert asked, "Do ye ken which stone?"

"Wait, there's more." Chris got up and poured himself a cup of coffee. "Beira has tasked me with freeing this friend, like one of those legends about sending the poor, love-struck squire off to prove himself worthy of the princess's hand. Very Culhwch and Olwen."

"Cull who and Olwen?" I asked.

"'Tis a Welsh romance about a hero besotted with a giant's daughter," Robert said.

Chris tipped his coffee cup toward Robert. "That's the one."

"Christopher, that's not what she'd doing," Anya said. Chris ignored her.

"So that's why I went to see Ethan last night, to get a bit of insight on these sort of stories," Chris said. "Do either of you have any idea how I can get a woman out of a boulder?"

"Perhaps," Robert replied. "Anya, d'ye ken what happened with your mum's friend?"

"It all happened long before I came along," Anya began, "but Mum has often spoken of her friend Meg. She was a giantess, and at the time she and Mum were friends, a local wizard had taken to accepting coin to trap giants in stone."

Robert grunted. "Long Meg?"

"Aye, that's her," Anya replied. "She was trapped in a standing circle a few hours south of here."

"If me memory serves me, Meg was trapped by a wizard called Scot," Robert said. "Michael Scot."

"If that's the man responsible, then Chris is off the hook," I said. "We don't have a relative by that name."

Chris coughed. "Actually, we do. That was one of Uncle John's aliases. Mom referred to it as his criminal name."

"Oh." I'd had no idea that Uncle John was a criminal, but I'd been a kid when he used to come around. I pursed my lips and looked at Robert. "Then that was him," I said. "We really did see my Uncle John hanging out with the Wild Court."

Chris set down his coffee. "What?"

"Robert and I went back to Aberfoyle," I replied. "Remember the tree on top of Doon Hill? It's like a portal to Elphame."

Chris grimaced. "Yeah, I remember."

"Well, what none of us realized back then was that I created the portal, and since I didn't know I was a walker I never closed it," I continued. "Fairies have been coming over from Elphame ever since. They were all over the hill."

"Was Nicnevin there?" Chris asked.

"We didn't see her," I replied. "But we did see Uncle John."

"How is that even possible?" Chris asked. "And are you sure it was John? I haven't seen him since I was in high school. Not since... before."

When Robert and Anya both looked confused, I said, "He means before our parents died." I thought for a moment. "Was Uncle John even at their funeral?"

"No. He wasn't. Based on the epic fight he had with Mom the last time he came around, if he had attended she probably would have sat up in her casket and slapped him."

"Mom got in a fight with someone?" Our mother had been quiet, polite, and avoided confrontation like the plague. An actual argument would have kicked her anxiety into overdrive. "About what?"

"John came by looking for money, same as always," Chris replied. "He'd run up another huge gambling debt. When he asked Dad for a loan, Mom just about threw him out of the house. Told him not to come back until he'd gotten treatment for his gambling addiction, and had transformed himself into a useful member of society."

"Wow." I sat back in my chair. "Okay, let's assume that Uncle John did turn Meg into stone."

"Rina, how—" Chris began, but I held up a hand.

"Table that, for now. It seems that the more pressing problem is un-stoning Meg, not figuring out how she got that way in the first place."

"That, and the door on Doon Hill," Robert added.

"Yeah. We'll work on that too." I opened my laptop and clicked around the internet until I found a page all about Long Meg and her stone circle. "Meg's in Cumbria, which is..." I typed the location into my phone's GPS app. "It's in a different country, for starters. Meg's in jolly old England."

Chris leaned over my shoulder, and looked at the map and directions on my screen. "A short three and a half hour drive. I can leave for England tomorrow. I'd go now, but my car's getting delivered tomorrow morning, and I'll need to sign for it."

"All right." I leaned across the table and grabbed a notepad and pencil. "We can hit the market and grab some food and bottled waters for the trip."

"Actually, I think only I should make this trip," Chris said. "That way, you two can work on the Doon Hill situation."

"And Uncle John?" I asked. Chris grimaced and turned away.

"Rina, I really don't want to see him. Besides, Beira told me to fix this, not ask you to handle it." He turned toward Anya. "Will you tell Beira I'm working on helping Meg?"

"Of course," Anya said a bit too quickly. "You know I will."

Chris nodded, then he turned away from her. Anya's face fell.

"It's settled, then. After I sign for my car, I'll take the rental and head down to Cumbria."

"You won't take your own car?" I asked.

"Before I can drive it, I need to report it to customs," he replied. "Then there will be the matter of getting plates and insurance." He stood and pushed in his chair. "If you'll excuse me, I have to work on some things my agent sent over. I'll be in my room for a bit."

With that, Chris went into his room and shut the door. Anya stared at it for a moment, then she turned around and left the cottage.

"That wasn't awkward at all," I said. "What the hell happened between those two?"

"Beira happened," Robert replied. "Wherever the Cailleach Bheur walks, she leaves her mark, be it on the land or on a man."

"Great. We just left behind one batch of mentally unstable gods and now we've run into more."

"'Tis worse now," Robert said. "This time, the god in question is family."

SOMETHING ROTTEN

S hutting my bedroom door on Anya was one of the hardest things
I've ever done. It was a mean, petty thing to do, but after she'd
abandoned me at the pub, I was feeling rather mean and petty. Add to
those wonderful emotions the sensation of abject stupidity, and I was
a trifecta of misery. I reasoned that I could wallow in these emotions,
or I could find a way to distract myself. Unfortunately, the only other
situation that needed my attention wasn't much better.

My suitcase was still resting next to the bed, exactly where I'd left it
before I'd gone out yesterday. I put it on the bed and retrieved my laptop and a notebook, and steeled myself for the other misery-inducing
situation I was dealing with. That task had nothing to do with fairies,
but with my latest novel's contract negotiations.

Honestly, I'd much rather deal with fairies.

I'd finished my promised novel, *Second Best Bed*, in record time
and had delivered it to my agent a week before I left New York. Once
I'd turned in that draft, I'd finally deposited the advance check the
publisher had drafted, since having a book in its nascent stages of
production made me feel as if I'd earned the money. I wondered now
if I shouldn't have cashed the check, since that made the contract a
bit more valid—the advance being the consideration portion of the

legalese—and therefore made my publisher's lawyers take a second look at the paperwork.

The publisher wasn't considering cancelling the contract; at least, my agent hadn't mentioned a cancellation. What did concern them was the fact that for the first three novels I'd released with them, I'd been an American citizen living on American soil, but for the fourth book I would be living in the United Kingdom. The fact that I remained an American citizen with an American bank account were apparently just details.

"Does anyone really need to know where I live? Do readers even care about that?" I'd asked my agent, Maisie, the day before I'd left. My apartment had already been packed and most of my belongings picked up by the moving company. "I'm sure any semi-competent accountant can work out whatever tax issues arise."

"It's not about the money," Maisie had said, and I knew she wasn't telling me everything. With my publisher, it was always about money. "They're concerned with how things look."

"What do you mean, look?" When she hadn't replied right away, I added, "I imagine it will look like I reside in a picturesque fishing village in Scotland. Come on, I can't be the first or only author they've published who lives overseas."

"You're not, but after the scandal with Olivia, you fleeing the country seems like an admission of guilt."

I enjoyed her mentioning how my ex-fiancée had sued me for plagiarism about as much as I enjoyed root canals. "Fleeing? How am I fleeing? I can't work at Carson University right now, since it was damaged during the winter break. My sister owns a house in Scotland and has invited me to stay with her. How is that fleeing?"

"Maybe we could just not tell anyone you're relocating."

"Yes, because lying is always the best way to correct things," I'd said. "Listen, Maisie, if you don't want to represent me any longer, it's fine. Just send me a release letter and I'll sign it."

I'd hung up after that, feeling terrified and exhilarated after possibly firing my agent. In the greater scheme of things that had been a dumb move on my part; Maisie was an excellent and sought after agent who knew her stuff and would fight for her clients. I suppose that's why it stung so badly when she seemed to give up on me. But Anya had been there, and her warm skin and soft lips had lessened the hurt.

I had nothing to soothe any of my hurts when I read the latest round of emails from Maisie, and Maisie's boss, and then the owner of the agency. I was now certain that hanging up on Maisie had not been my best move. What was interesting was how badly the agency wanted to keep me on, despite Maisie's earlier cautions.

I got up and grabbed the bottle of Scotch that had been sitting on my nightstand, twisted off the cap, and took a swig. I assumed the caretaker, Dougal, had left it for me, and if he was the sort of caretaker who cut grass and supplied liquor, I wanted to extend his contract for the next decade. I took a second drink as I scrolled through my emails, and found one that had come from my publisher directly. That was odd, since most of the messages from them were filtered through my agent, even editorial questions.

I opened the email, and read a pithy yet encouraging message from my editor:

"Hello Mr. Stewart,

I'm quite pleased with the draft you've submitted and have sent it on to the editing pool. We will be in touch soon."

Huh. There weren't any "what are you doing in Scotland" or "your new address will upset our corporate reporting guidelines" comments in the message, almost as if they didn't care where I lived so long as I submitted quality work.

I settled myself against the headboard, keeping the Scotch within easy reach, my laptop balanced on my knees as I started researching my agency. Specifically, I wanted to know if any authors had filed complaints against them, and what their complaints were about. Something was rotten, and this time it wasn't in Denmark.

WELCOME FROM THE KING

With Chris hiding in his room and Anya off in the village delivering a message to her mother, Robert and I passed the time by unpacking our suitcases. There wasn't a lot to unpack, since we'd shipped over most of what we owned, which meant that over half of our stuff was still on its way to Scotland; right now it was all stowed away on one of those boats Robert had wanted to travel on instead of an airplane. And even those crates wouldn't amount to much, since neither Robert nor I owned much more than clothes, books, and rock specimens—okay, the rocks were all mine—and the few pieces of furniture that had lived in my apartment weren't worth the cost or bother of shipping. Luckily, the cottage had come furnished.

Chris had shipped over a dozen crates, filled with furniture, books, and who knows what else. I wondered where we'd fit all of Chris's stuff when it arrived. Hopefully, there was a storage facility nearby.

I'd just unpacked my favorite ammonite fossil and set it on the shelf next to the cornucopia when Robert unzipped my second suitcase. "I see ye were careful to pack all the important items," he said with a smile.

Even though I'd packed that case myself, I wandered over and peeked at the contents. Robert had found my stash of geology texts. "I might need references," I said. "We still haven't done that walking trail in the Trossachs. What if we find more fossils? I'll need to be able to identify them."

"Aye, ye do love your wee stone beasties." Robert picked up the books and brought them to the bookcase. He said something else about the Trossachs, but I hardly heard him. Underneath the geology texts were several pregnancy books.

I'd never told Robert I'd bought them. I'd gotten them at a local bookstore and paid for all of the books in cash out of concern that if I ordered them online and they were delivered while I wasn't home, he would worry something was wrong with me or the baby. Not that Robert would ever open a package that wasn't addressed to him, or fault me for doing research. The worst part was that even though I'd devoured every word in those books and several others, I still hadn't found the answers I was looking for.

"What are these?" Robert asked when he caught me staring. He picked up one of the books and flipped through the pages. "Studyin' to be a midwife, are ye?"

"No. I..." My voice wavered, and I bit my lip. "That elixir you get from Fionnlagh? What's in it?"

Robert put down the book. "What's wrong?"

"N-Nothing!"

He took my hands. "Love, 'tis plain that something is."

"Nothing. Really. It's just..." I pulled away from Robert and scrubbed my face with my hands. "It's just that over the past few decades we've learned about an awful lot about things that can harm a fetus and you said the elixir is made from wine and alcohol can build up in the placenta and I'm worried that it might hurt Faith."

"All right, then. I shall ask the king what the elixir is comprised of."

Robert was so calm in the face of my freak out, he caught me off guard. "You will?"

"O' course I will. I canna have a wee dram harmin' ye or our bairn."

"It won't."

Robert and I turned toward the voice. Fionnlagh himself was standing in the center of the cottage in his full Seelie King regalia: leather cape, antlered headdress, and all. I hoped the headdress's prongs wouldn't scratch the ceiling.

"My lord," Robert said. "Thank you."

The corner of Fionnlagh's mouth curled up. "For what? For eavesdropping on a private conversation between you and your bride? If the situation were reversed, I would not be thanking you."

"You're sure?" I asked. "The elixir won't hurt my baby?"

"I am certain, walker," he replied. "Even if there had been an ingredient that would have done you harm, I'd have a potion brewed to counteract it. Rest assured, now that you have returned to my island, you are both under my protection." His gaze travelled to the cornucopia, and he frowned slightly. "I see many gods have offered you such boons."

"Is it wrong for me to have the cornucopia here in Scotland?" I asked. "I didn't mean to offend you."

"You haven't. A walker never owes allegiance to one god or land. Rather, they move between and work wherever they're needed."

Interesting. "Oh. Okay. Thank you."

"My visit today was meant to welcome you," Fionnlagh said. "Now that you are both on Scotland's soil perhaps things will return to the way they're meant to be."

"'Tis good to be home," Robert said. "And to be in such a fine home, at that."

"The home is yours, now and forever. My only request is that you fill it with children."

I felt my face warm. "We're working on that."

"Good." With that, Fionnlagh bowed his head and faded from view. I collapsed against Robert, and let his strong arms wrap around me while I shuddered with relief.

"Why aren't you telling me I freaked out over nothing?" I asked.

"Did ye worry I would chastise ye for your concern o'er our bairn?" Robert set his hands on the sides of my face and held my gaze with his. "Nothing in heaven or earth is more important to me than the two o' ye. Nothing."

Tears were coursing down my face. Robert wiped my cheeks with his thumbs and drew me against his chest. "I will do anything to keep ye safe. Ye can be sure o' that."

"Crap. We should have asked Fionnlagh about Dougal."

"We'll ask when next we see him. Do no' fash, love. We ha' plenty o' time."

After I'd calmed down, Robert went out to pick up lunch. Normally I would have gone with him, but I was still shaky. No sooner had the door closed behind Robert than Chris emerged from his room.

He sat next to me on the couch and turned on the television. While he flipped through the channels I grabbed a throw blanket and burrowed underneath it.

"Not sharing is mean," Chris said.

"Fine." I tossed a corner of the blanket onto his leg. "Did you hear?"

"I did." Chris went past a black and white movie, and then a golf tournament. "You can talk to me, you know."

"I know." I worried the edge of the blanket. "What happened with Anya?"

"What makes you think anything happened with Anya?"

"She isn't here and you smell like Scotch."

He put down the remote. "When I went to meet her at the pub, Beira jumped down my throat the moment she saw me, and Anya did nothing. *Nothing*. She didn't say anything, or do anything, or even stick around to talk to me afterwards."

"Wow." That was pretty harsh, especially for someone as warm and loving as Anya. "Did you ask her why?"

"No. I didn't even see her again until this morning when she showed up here." Chris looked at the ceiling. "I get that she values her mother's opinion, but the way she just sat there, not even trying to defend me... It was like I didn't mean anything to her."

"Like when Olivia just up and left, and didn't even take her engagement ring?"

Chris's gaze slid toward me. "Have I mentioned how much I hate that you remember everything that has ever happened to both of us?" He blew out a breath and rubbed his eyes. "Yeah. That's exactly how it felt."

"Then I think you need to figure out if Anya's worth feeling this way," I said. "For the longest time, you were convinced that Olivia was the last woman you'd ever love. Do you feel that way about Anya?"

"Yes. No. I don't know. All I know is that what I feel for Anya is like nothing I've ever felt before." He was silent for a moment. "Is that how you feel about Robert?"

"I can truthfully say that Robert is not the last woman I will ever love."

"If you weren't pregnant, I'd smack you."

"Like Robert says, our Faith will guide us."

Chris groaned, and went back to channel flipping. After a moment, I said, "For what it's worth, I think Anya is worth fighting for."

"Yeah. Me too."

RIGHTEOUS

The shipping contractor delivered my car to the cottage just before eight a.m. the next morning, right on time and without a scratch on her. In fact, she was so clean I wondered if they'd washed her along the way.

As my car was lowered down off the flatbed trailer, I felt like some things in my life had settled. Beira's long-held grudge had blindsided me, as did my uncle's possible reappearance and Anya's strange and disconcerting behavior. But now my car was here, and much like the reappearance of an old friend, I had a bit of my normal life back. The BMW's sleek chassis was certainly out of place in rustic Crail, and since she was constructed for an American market, the driver's seat was on the wrong side for UK roads, but I didn't care about little things like that. She was here, and I was ecstatic.

"I can't wait to take her out on these country roads," I said. The flatbed had departed, and I was admiring how the paint job sparkled in the early morning light.

Rina glanced at me and raised an eyebrow. She'd always thought I was unnaturally attached to my car, but what did she know? She hardly ever drove. "The sheep will never know what hit them. Literally."

"As if I'd let a sheep's woolly ass anywhere near her," I said. "That paint color—"

"I know all about your custom ultraviolet paint job," Rina said over me. "Just be careful, okay?"

"I will." I looped my arm around her neck and gave her one of those awkward big brother hugs. "I'll call you when I get there."

"You better. I put the cooler with your lunch in the rental's back seat."

It was a supreme piece of irony that my car had arrived, yet I would take the compact rental on this road trip to visit Long Meg. "You are the best sister I've ever had, no doubt about it."

Rina smacked my shoulder. "Since I'm your only sister, I guess I'm also the worst."

"Your words, not mine."

I said my goodbyes to Rina and Rob, then I took the rental car's keys and a map and headed south toward Cumbria. It was still rather early, and I was hoping to reach the English border by noon. As I drove away from the cottage and down the hill, I felt like a character in a badly researched historical movie setting out on a quest. To make matters worse, I was in search of a giant.

Crap, this isn't even a big budget film. I'm in a Monty Python sketch. I laughed, and drummed my hands against the steering wheel, desperately hoping to find humor in the absurdity of it all. Standing at the intersection where our driveway met the main road was Anya, her yellow hair shining in the morning light.

She was wearing a dress, which she hardly ever did; if anything, Anya was a jeans and boots kind of girl, and I loved that about her. But there she was, standing on the side of the road wearing a red dress patterned with white flowers, the breeze kicking her skirts up past her knees. A simple thing like an article of clothing shouldn't mean so much, but it did. I wondered if Anya had put it on to make amends, or say goodbye.

I almost drove right by her. Who did she think she was, disappearing on me not once but twice, and now showing up out of the blue and dressed like we were going on a date and almost causing a traffic accident? But I was going through with this whole ridiculous quest for her, because I could no longer imagine my life without her in it. Imagining my life without Beira looming over us, now that I could do.

I stopped the car, then I leaned over and opened the passenger door. Anya got in, and I turned onto the main road.

"You're angry with me," she said.

"I've been happier."

And we drove on, speeding past green hills and rolling meadows. It was a beautiful day for driving, ideal for a romantic outing. Too bad the woman beside me seemed to have lost all interest in romance, at least with me.

"You could have warned me that your mother hated me," I said.

"I didn't have the slightest idea, not until a few days ago," Anya cried. "My mum has always spoken highly of Karina. I'd had no idea your family was in any way affiliated with mine."

She was right; Beira did hold Rina in high regard, so much so that she had sent her only daughter to protect her from Demeter's crazed plans. So why had the Stewarts been good people then, but were bad people now?

Me. The answer was me.

"Face it, Anya, your mother doesn't want you to be with me," I said. "That's what this all comes down to. Not a friend turned to stone, not a giantess and her bones. It's a simple case of me not being good enough for you."

"That is not true," Anya said.

"Isn't it?" I countered. "It sure feels that way. It did when you sat there next to me and didn't say a word while Beira berated me and my entire family, and it really did when you disappeared before we could talk about it. Do you do everything she tells you to do? Do you even have a mind of your own?"

Anya remained silent. After a minute or so, I glanced toward her, and saw her staring out the passenger side window.

"Why am I doing this?" I asked. "Three days ago, you loved me. Now you won't even look at me. What the hell do I care if Beira approves of me? It's not her opinion that matters."

My voice caught at the end. I swallowed hard and concentrated on the road.

"Why are you doing this?" Anya asked.

"If I had any sense I wouldn't even attempt it," I began. "What do I know about wizards and stone giantesses? Nothing, that's what. But Beira said my family wronged yours, so I at least have to learn about the situation and do what I can. It's what my father would have done."

"He was a proud man?"

"Not proud. Righteous. His moral compass always pointed north. If he thought he or our family was in any way responsible for something wrong, he'd move heaven and earth to fix it."

Anya laughed softly. "He was a good man, then. As are you."

I thought of a hundred crass retorts. Before I could put words to my thoughts, Anya reached over the center console and touched my hand. I was so startled I almost went into a ditch.

"Gods, haven't you driven before?" Anya shrieked.

"On the right side of the road," I said as I swerved back onto the paved lane. "Literally."

I realized we were smiling at each other. "Anya, why are you here now?"

"You impressed Mum, and that's no mean feat," she replied. "She expected that you'd run to the gallowglass, and that he would put to rights whatever your uncle had done. When I told her that you alone were going south to see what could be done about Meg, she was speechless." Anya flashed me a grin. "Can you make her speechless more often? Now that would be a fine trick."

I laughed, despite that I was still hurt. "Why didn't you say anything to defend me at the pub? And why did you leave?"

Anya looked at her hands, folded in her lap. "It's not easy being the Queen of Winter's daughter. I suppose it's not easy being one of her sons, either, but I have many brothers. I'm the only lass in the household." Her hands unfolded and folded together again. "She worries for me, doesn't want to see me hurt."

"Anya, I've watched you fight gods."

"True. You have. And the only time Mum's ever seen me weep was when a boy broke my heart."

My own heart ached, and I felt like I understood Beira a bit more than I had. She only wanted to see her daughter happy, and Beira's definition of happiness probably didn't include a mortal who'd recently been in bed with the Seelie Queen.

I reached over and grasped Anya's hand. "You know I won't hurt you. Not ever."

She wound her fingers with mine. "Aye. I ken that."

THE TOASTER STAYS

After Chris went south to check out Long Meg in her natural
habitat, Robert and I celebrated having the cottage all to ourselves by making toast and oatmeal for breakfast. Living in the fast
lane, that was us.

What was a bit more interesting was how we'd come by the aforementioned toast and oatmeal. When the car delivery people had
knocked on our door at oh dark thirty in the morning, they alerted us
to a cooler that was resting on our front stoop. Inside said cooler was
an assortment of groceries, including the bread and sliced turkey that
had ended up as Chris's road trip sandwiches. (Yes, I endured the meat
stink. He is my brother, after all.) It was like the food elves had decided
to favor us with a visit, though I assumed a certain phooka was the one
responsible. Not that that fact kept me from enjoying my breakfast.

"We should be grateful we have any food in the house at all," I said,
as I heaped butter and brown sugar into my bowl of oatmeal. "Dougal
must have gone shopping for us. That was nice."

Robert grunted, then he got up from the table and started an
argument with the toaster. "You're going to break it," I warned when
he slammed the lever down so hard it shook.

"Blasted machines," he grumbled. "Our home is filled wi' such devices. Why can't we just build a fire for warmth and cooking?"

"Can you even make toast over a fire?" I asked. "Wouldn't the bread burn up?"

"O' course ye can," Robert replied. "Ye can make any food ye desire wi' no more than a fire and a good iron pot. It's the way things were done for centuries, but now we are dependent on these... these..."

The toast popped up. I watched as Robert grabbed the slices, mutter a curse when he burned his fingers, and drop the toast onto his plate. He left everything to cool as he stalked toward the electric kettle.

"We could boil water o'er a fire," he said. "We could keep a kettle at the ready all day and night."

"We could not," I said as I walked past him toward the kitchen sink. "Mainly because we don't have a wood burning fireplace."

Robert cast his glare onto the great room. There was an electric fire in the living area, but it was fully enclosed and more for aesthetics than heat. A modern central heating system was what actually kept the cottage warm.

"I will build us a proper hearth," Robert declared. "Then we can do away with these metal contraptions and live as God intended."

"I like these metal contraptions." I rinsed off the butter knife, then I faced him and crossed my arms over my chest. "And I for one do not think I was put on this earth to spend sixteen hours of the day cooking and beating laundry on a rock in the river. The toaster stays."

Robert's gaze darted between me and the toaster. For a moment, I thought he was going to argue with me.

"Listen, if you want a fireplace that badly go ahead and build one, but on one condition."

"What's that, now?"

I stepped closer and took his hands. "Tell me why you're so upset."

Robert's anger and frustration visibly deflated, and he leaned his forehead against mine. "I do no' like that MacKay has been here again."

"You were all right with us borrowing his truck."

"The truck was a necessity, but I do no' want him in our home."

"He was just on the front stoop."

"That is near enough."

"You hate him that much?"

"I do no' hate anything or anyone, but that one is a trickster," Robert replied. "I do no' want him near us, or our bairn."

My blood went cold. "Do you really think he was sent to watch us? Or maybe hurt Faith?"

"I have no idea, but I mean to find out."

I shivered. Robert wrapped his arms around me. I appreciated his affections, but I wasn't shivering from the cold.

"Fear not, Karina me love," he said against my hair. "I shall protect ye and Faith with my body and sword. Whatever tricks MacKay has planted, they will bear no fruit. You are both safe."

"I know." I burrowed deeper into his arms. The combination of his warm body and the warm oatmeal in my belly was making me sleepy. "Let's go back to bed."

Robert drew back and looked at me, his brow pinched. "We just got out o' bed."

"I know, but it's not like we have anything we need to do right now. We can lay down, and relax, and you can tell me all about how you used to cook like a caveman over open flames." I paused to yawn. "Besides, I need a nap."

"All right, love." Robert picked up his cup of tea, and we walked toward our bedroom. "Karina?"

"Yes?"

"Do ye care for the toaster more than me?"

"Don't be silly. Of course I don't." I kicked off my slippers and sat on the bed. "The coffeemaker, now that's a different story."

When I woke I was alone in bed. The sunlight hadn't moved too far across the floor, which told me I hadn't slept for very long. I sat up and stretched, then I went out to the kitchen. There was a full pot of coffee waiting for me on the counter. I wondered if Robert had thought I was serious about liking the coffeemaker more than him.

As I poured coffee into a mug, I glanced out to the back garden, and saw Robert practicing swordplay as the wights fluttered around him like a spray of confetti. Robert had stripped off his shirt, and sweat shone on his well-toned upper body. I briefly wondered why he was practicing outside half-naked in March while the frigid winds still howled across the countryside. After a moment, I put that question aside and enjoyed the show. It was a good thing we had a walled garden, or the sight of a shirtless man with a giant sword might have made the neighbors nervous, or at least curious.

I went out to the garden, mug of coffee in hand and a bottle of water in my jacket pocket. When Robert saw me he paused in his routine.

"I see you got bored with our nap," I said as I tossed him the water bottle.

Robert grinned as he twisted off the cap. "I see ye did no' mind watchin' me for a bit."

I grinned right back at him. "I have a question."

"Ask away, love."

"One thing I've never understood is how the scholarly Reverend Kirk had time to learn how to wield a sword well enough to become the gallowglass. Weren't you busy with your translations, and with the church?"

"Aye, I was busy with all that and more. Still, 'twas a different time then and I'd learned how to handle a blade when I was a boy."

"Defending the homestead against bandits?"

"That was the idea, at any rate, and you are correct, I had nowhere near the skill I have today. Then I was sent to oversee the kirk in Aberfoyle, and I found me way Underhill."

"Wait. You mean the fairies taught you how to fight?"

"Not quite." He picked up his sword and completed a few flourishes; while I'd never heard him outright brag about his skill, he did like showing off now and then. "When I'd spend the evening at their revels, I watched the tournaments. As I observed fighters far more skilled than I was, I learned. The more I watched and learned, the better swordsman I was meself. Then the day came when Nicnevin took me, and I spent all day and night watchin' them as they drank, and danced, and fought."

"I bet you learned a few things then."

"That I did, love. Believe me, none of it prepared me for when she pitted me against her gallowglass, and I won." Robert lowered his sword and regarded the blade. "Even after all these years, I'm still shocked."

"We weren't shocked," came a man's voice. I turned toward it and saw Dougal standing at the garden's gate. "We in the audience knew you'd be victorious," Dougal continued as he stepped into the garden. Some of the wights fluttered onto his shoulders, but I noticed Wyatt remained near Robert.

"Here again, are ye?" Robert thrust his sword into the ground and took a step toward Dougal. "Whose home is this, yours or mine?"

"Do ye speak to all guests this way?" Dougal countered.

"Are ye a guest or an intruder?" Robert crossed his arms over his chest. "That question has yet to be answered."

"Thank you for the food," I said in a rush. "That was from you, wasn't it?"

"Aye, 'twas me, and you're quite welcome, Mistress Stewart." Dougal faced Robert. "As I was sayin', your predecessor was a right scoundrel, and made enemies wherever he went. Many were pleased when he fell."

"What sort of a being is pleased by death?" Robert demanded. "A soulless one, to be sure."

Dougal only shrugged. I took a few steps toward Robert; I had no idea what an angry phooka was capable of, and I did not want to find out. "Why have you come by?" I asked. "Is there something we can help you with?"

"I was coming by to help ye," Dougal said. "Ye have seen what's become o' the hill?"

"Hill?" I repeated.

"Doon Hill," Dougal clarified. "I know ye took me truck there."

"Um, yeah. Sorry about that, but my brother took our car."

"No worries. I left it for ye, should ye need transport. Now, have ye any idea what's to be done about it?"

"Done?" I asked, while Robert demanded, "Why have ye truly come here today?"

"As I said, to offer a bit o' help to ye," Dougal said, smiling as if the gallowglass wasn't a hair's breadth from ripping his throat out. "It seems to me that ye need to close the door ye left open. Wedge it shut, if ye will. Have ye any idea how to do that?"

"We're working on it," I hedged. "Why? Did someone send you to check up on us?"

"No' as much, but I can tell ye that Nicnevin is no' pleased that half o' her court has dwindled away."

Robert snorted. "Ye would still be associated with that foul court."

Dougal smiled and spread his hands. "Were ye no' her subject as well for o'er three centuries? I daresay ye ken more about her court than I do."

Robert jerked toward Dougal, but I stayed him with a hand on his arm. "Well, thanks for that bit of information. We'll get working on it right away."

"I knew ye would, lass. Feel free to use the truck, or me toolbox, if ye ha' need o' it." He turned to go, then added, "Oh, and the lady is in quite a state. It seems she can no' locate her daughter."

"Nicnevin has a daughter?" I asked.

Robert shook his head. "He means Beira. And no, we've no idea where Anya's got to. If we see her, we'll tell her to contact her mum straight aways."

Dougal tipped his cap. "Noble as ever, gallowglass. I shall pass the message along."

With that, Dougal left the courtyard. When I didn't hear an engine start up I followed him and saw his truck parked where I'd left it after we'd returned from Aberfoyle. That's when I realized that I hadn't heard a car pull up, either.

"How does he get around?" I wondered.

"Best not to think too much on him," Robert said as he walked past me and entered the cottage. "Like as no' 'twill give ye a headache."

"Ugh," I said as I rubbed my temples. "That's the last thing I need."

A GRAVEYARD FOR GIANTS

"Long Meg sure is...long."

"Of course she is," Anya said. "She is a giantess, after all."

I glanced at Anya, then back to the boulder that was Long Meg. In her present state, she was a twelve foot tall hunk of red sandstone situated in the middle of a farmer's field. Someone had carved swirling lines and concentric circles onto Meg's surface, and according to my research, the four corners of the stone lined up perfectly with the compass points. Whoever had set Meg in place had done so with precision and purpose.

Huh. I wondered if the stone was twelve feet tall because that was how tall Meg was. As Anya said, she was a giantess.

About eighty feet away from Meg was a corresponding stone circle, which was commonly referred to as Long Meg's daughters. It was comprised of over fifty additional granite boulders, and made up a lopsided oval that extended north toward a ditch. The circle was also full of cows, which I assumed belonged to the nearby farm. I was not expecting an audience of livestock while we examined the area; then again, I'd had no idea of what to expect. Giants and wizards were new territory for me.

For what felt like the hundredth time, I wished I hadn't asked Rina and Rob to stay home. Rina would have loved all of these rocks, and Rob would have had some insights on the local lore. I could barely wrap my head around how a living, breathing creature could possibly have been turned into stone. But my sister and brother-in-law weren't here, so I pressed onward as best I could.

"Do you know why she was turned to stone?" I asked.

Anya shook her head. "I've heard rumors and such, nothing more—but Meg wasn't turned to stone. The stones were already here, and the wizard trapped her inside."

That answered one question, and created about a hundred more. "How is she still alive in there?" I reached out and touched the cold, damp stone. "Is there a way to tell?"

Anya shrugged. "Like as not, she's in a magically induced stasis."

"Like as not," I muttered. "So, what you're saying is that she has no idea about all the time that's passed while she's been in there, or that she's stuck in a rock in the middle of a farmer's field? Does she even know we're standing in front of her?"

Anya smiled, and it was as if the sun had come out from behind a cloud. "We can ask her ourselves once she's free."

Her confidence in me being able to help Meg meant more to me than every accolade and fan letter my writing had received over the years. I wanted to pull Anya into my arms and then down to the grass and show her how much it meant, but before any of that could happen, there was work to be done. Not only did we have to somehow free Meg from the stone, Anya and I needed to figure out if our relationship was salvageable.

"Yeah, about freeing her. Now that I've met Meg, I can openly and honestly admit that I have no idea how to get her out of there." I ran a hand through my hair, then I checked my watch; it was after three, which meant we'd been at this for hours. "Did you pack a bag?"

Anya blinked. "A bag of what?"

"Clothes. You know, an overnight bag."

"I did not realize we'd be staying the night."

"I didn't either, but I like to be prepared. Come on." I started walking back toward the car, and Anya fell into step beside me.

"Where are we going?" she asked.

"I need to think, and I do my best thinking on a full stomach." I held open the passenger door. After Anya was inside the car, I went around to the driver's side. "I also think better after I've relaxed a bit, therefore my current plan is to find a nice hotel, book us a room, and grab a bite to eat."

"What of the all the food your sister packed?"

"We finished that an hour ago."

"Still, you don't need to pay for a room," Anya said. "I can transport us home in the blink of an eye."

"What about the car?"

She frowned. "I've never tried to move a vehicle."

"While I have complete faith in your abilities, I'd rather not have you use our rental car as a guinea pig. If anything goes wrong, I doubt the insurance will cover it." I pulled onto the main road and headed toward a town called Penrith. "What do you say? Want to have dinner with me?"

There was that smile again. "I'd love to."

It wasn't long before I found us a hotel. It was a repurposed seventeenth century manor house, and from the road it looked like every one of the stock images of British country estates splashed across American travel magazines. The hotel itself was built from pale gray stone, and a vast, well-manicured lawn rolled right up to the entrance. A formal knot garden sat off to the side, and signs pointed to a hedge maze out back. Despite the lush surroundings the rooms weren't too expensive—they weren't as cheap as they would have been in Scotland, but were far more reasonable than a hotel in London or even New York would have been—and those grounds were gorgeous, even in late winter.

After we'd checked in and cleaned up, Anya and I went to the hotel restaurant for an early dinner, or maybe it was a really late lunch. It was too late for lunch by British or American standards, but we weren't the only diners present. I supposed the hotel wanted to accommodate their guests and were used to serving people at odd hours.

The dining room itself walked a fine line between elegant and stuffy. The tables were covered with crisp white linen and laid out with more forks than any reasonable person would want or need for a simple lunch. Each one of the leather-bound and parchment menus—the spines were even decorated with gold tassels—probably cost more than a case of my books in hardcovers. But the staff was friendly, and they smiled whenever the patrons in the bar started belting out a new song.

"You said you've heard rumors about Meg?" I asked after the server went to fetch our drinks. "Tell them to me."

"What good will repeating rumors do?" Anya asked.

I shrugged. "Who knows? Maybe it won't accomplish anything, but most stories have at least one thread of truth holding them together. If we find Meg's thread and give it a good tug, we might unravel the whole situation."

"Very well." Anya unfolded her napkin and spread it across her lap. "Some tales say that Meg was a witch who was turned to stone along with her coven."

"About that coven. Did they become Meg's Daughters?" I asked, referring to the stone circle.

"Aye, that's correct. They say a man came across them one night dancing under the moonlight, and made a few indecent requests. When they told him to take a hike, he got in a huff and set them in stone."

"And you're certain that the man who did this is somehow related to me?"

"Aye. That John Damian has been going all around the island telling anyone who will listen that the walker is his niece, and offering his services against any remaining giants. How the Seelie Court hasn't yet caught up to him is a mystery."

I swallowed hard. "He knows about Rina?"

Anya gave me a look. "Everyone knows about Karina and the gallowglass."

The server returned with our drinks and took our order. After she left, I pulled out a brochure about the local area I'd grabbed from the front desk. I'd picked it up because it had the word 'giant' printed right on the front page.

"It seems that there are quite a few mentions of giants around here," I said. "We've got a Giant's Grave, Giant's Thumb, and even some caves where giants supposedly live."

Anya nodded. "This land is something of a graveyard for giants."

I froze with my glass halfway to my mouth. "You mean some of these legends are true?"

"Of course they are. One of the few ways to contain a giant is to encase him in stone. Since this area was already so rich with boulders and monuments, it's where most of my kind ended up after a run-in with a rogue wizard or two."

My kind. "Anya, is your father a giant?"

"Aye."

"He wasn't, ah, too big for Beira?"

"Am I too big for you?"

"I'm beginning to think I'm too small for your mother."

"Christopher—"

"Forget it," I said, making a shooing motion with my hand. "I'm sorry. That was petty."

Our food arrived soon enough, and Anya and I ate in silence for a few minutes. "You didn't tell me what you thought was the truth of Meg."

"Our family has our own tale about Meg," Anya replied. "According to Mum, your relation fancied Meg, not only for her body but also for her power. When she said turned him down—repeatedly—he set her in stone and took her power regardless."

"That's terrible," I said. It also fit my uncle to a tee. He was always trying to connive people out of something, or rope them into his latest get rich quick scheme.

"So he takes Meg's power, changes his name, and then...what?" I paused for a bite of lamb. It had been prepared with honey and some kind of pepper, and it was amazing. "I researched Michael Scot last night. If my uncle is the same person, he's over eight-hundred-years-old."

Anya raised an eyebrow. "And?"

"And while I do not doubt your or your mother's word in the slightest, I can't reconcile how or why an eight-hundred-year-old wizard would somehow insinuate himself in my family."

Anya chewed thoughtfully for a moment. "Then perhaps the identity you need to research is that of John Damian, being that he's closer to you in time and space."

That was Anya, as intelligent as she was beautiful. "Perhaps you're right."

UNCLE JOHN

S ince I wasn't in the mood to shop or cook, Robert and I went out for lunch. It was a clear and sunny early spring day, and we wanted to take a walk around the village's ancient cobbled streets. We ended up at a tea room near the center of the village, and stuffed ourselves full of scones and jam and clotted cream. It wasn't the healthiest lunch, but it was very, very tasty.

When we admitted we couldn't eat another bite, the proprietors brought us a second round of steaming cups of tea. We lingered over them, watching the village go about its business through the large front windows. It was a perfect, lazy afternoon, until I recognized a certain man walking by the tea shop.

"Uncle John." I set down my cup and knocked on the window. "Robert, that's my uncle!"

Uncle John noticed me, or rather he noticed a crazy woman inside the tea room waving her arms and tapping on the window. After a moment, I saw recognition light up in his eyes, and I gestured for him to come inside.

"Karina," Robert said. "Is this wise?"

"Honestly, probably not." That was all I had time to say before John was standing at the edge of our table.

"Karina Stewart, James's lass?" John began. "Is it really you?"

"Sure is," I replied. "It's great to see you!"

"And you," he replied. "I haven't seen you since you were a wee thing. What are you doing here in Scotland?"

"I live here now," I replied. "Uncle John, this is Robert Kirk. We live here together."

Robert stood and extended his hand. "A pleasure, sir," he said as they shook hands. "Please, sit with us. Let me buy ye a cup o' tea."

"All right, then," John said. "It would be my pleasure."

John sat along the outer edge of the table. It was surreal, sitting with the man I'd thought was my regular old uncle up until I saw him hanging out with a bunch of wayward fairies on Doon Hill.

"So, ye reside here in Scotland," John said. "Have ye lived here long?"

"Technically, we've only lived here a few days," I replied. "I was here last summer, and we came back a few days ago."

"We?" John asked, his gaze darting toward Robert. "I take it the two o' ye met here?"

"We did," Robert replied. "In Aberfoyle, as a matter o' fact."

"Ah." John leaned back in his chair, and motioned to the server for a menu. "That does explain a few things. Tell me, Karina, how is your brother?"

"Chris is doing great," I replied. "He's a bestselling author now."

"I thought he was an English teacher?"

How would John even be aware of that? "He was, but not currently. What have you been up to these last fifteen or so years?"

"Oh, many things. Many, many things." The serve brought over a menu, and John looked it over. Speaking from experience, it wasn't nearly as fascinating as John pretended it was.

"What do you know o' the Seelie Court?" Robert demanded.

John looked at him over the top of his glasses. "Gallowglasses aren't ones for subtlety, are they now? I suppose I should have expected that."

I smiled at Robert. "They sure aren't," I said. "If you know about the Court, does that mean you also know about what Nicnevin did to Chris?"

John's face darkened. "Aye. Many were no' pleased with her treatment o' him. In fact," he leaned closer and pitched his voice low, "many wonder if Nicnevin is fit to rule at all."

"Those in doubt can look to Fionnlagh for leadership," Robert said.

John looked at Robert for a moment. "Loyal and outspoken, then. Two traits that do no' always pair well." He glanced at his wrist. "Will ye look at the time? Karina, Robert, it has been a pleasure." He stood, then he withdrew a card from his sleeve and dropped it on the table.

"Have dinner with me tonight," he said. "Both of ye. The address is on the card."

"Um, okay." I picked up the card; the address was right here in Crail. Coincidences just abounded. "What time?"

"Eight would be perfect. Until then!"

With that, John left the tea room. I watched him walk down a narrow side street until he turned a corner and was out of sight.

"What the hell just happened?" I asked.

"I finally met one o' your relations, other than Christopher, that's what." Robert looked over the check, then he put some money on the table. "Ready, love?"

"Sure." We put on our coats and went out into the brisk spring air. "Will we meet one of your relatives next?"

Robert snorted. "Now that would be an experience."

Hand in hand, we wandered the village streets. In time we reached the beach and kept going past the sea wall, then we stood together watching the waves. It was the same spot we'd stood in months ago, right before the *fuath* crawled up out of the ocean and tried to eat us.

"I'm glad there aren't any seals here this time," I said.

Robert nodded. "Me, as well."

"Do you think the *fuath* will ever some back?"

"In time, they surely will, and when they do, hopefully we won't be their prey." Robert put his arm around my shoulders. "I noticed that ye did no' tell your uncle about our bairn."

"No, I didn't." I kicked at a clump of wet sand. "I mean, what if he isn't really my uncle? What if he's some kind of demon that was sent to hurt us? Around here, anything can happen. I think that for now, at least, Faith is on a need to know basis."

"A sound plan, that is."

Once we were back at the cottage, Robert and I went into full research mode. The bookshelf in the cottage did not have any folklore or mythological offerings other than what we'd brought with us, but I did have my laptop and the whole of the internet at my disposal. Some of the information housed on the internet was even accurate. I searched online while Robert sat at my elbow, taking notes on everything we could find out about the historical John Damian.

"He was an alchemist," I announced after I'd clicked around the web for a bit. "He even worked for a king."

Robert leaned forward and read further down the page. "Says here the fool built himself a set o' wings and tried to fly out o' Stirling Castle. Landed in a midden, he did."

"How very Icarian of him. Or should that be Daedalusian?" When Robert drew back and regarded me with a shocked face, I said, "What? I know some legends, too."

"Ye surely are brilliant," he said, as he squeezed my shoulder.

"Too bad I'm not brilliant enough to figure out what's going on here."

"Perhaps we'll learn more at dinner."

"Do you think having dinner with him is a good idea?" I asked. "We don't have to go."

"But what will we learn if we don't?" Robert countered. "I believe it is our duty to discover all we can about him and this new court. Perhaps John will ken a way to close the door on Doon Hill once and for all."

"Maybe." I clicked on another article about the historical John Damian and scanned it. According to the author, John had been a notorious gambler as well as an unsuccessful alchemist. Chris would appreciate that bit of trivia. "If nothing else, having dinner with him will keep us from having to go to the market until tomorrow."

THE SOURCE OF THE SPELL

After Anya and I finished our lunch, we decided to take a walk around the town. The part of Cumbria we were staying in was rife with monuments with the word giant in the title, and I wanted to see a few of them in person. Lucky for us, many of these sites were within walking distance of the hotel.

There was also the fact that Anya and I were together, and while I was still mad at her for not speaking up while Beira had handed me my ass, at least I was with her. I'd gotten used to sleeping beside her, with her buttercup yellow hair spread across the pillows and tickling my nose in my dreams. During the few days when we were apart, I'd missed her so much it hurt, and truth be told, I was only on this quest for giants to try to appease her mother, and then get our relationship back to where we'd been. It had been a pretty good place.

More than anything, I wanted to do whatever needed to be done to save Meg, if for no other reason than to put this giant nonsense behind us. Part of me thought that was wishful thinking, and that no matter what happened with Meg, Beira would come up with new reasons to keep Anya and me apart. I guessed it was up to Anya to either stand up to her mother, or let the pattern continue. The rest of me wanted to tell Beira to put her opinions where the sun doesn't shine.

I wondered what happened to those who mouthed off to the Queen of Winter.

"Here's the church," Anya said.

Before we'd started our walk, I'd grabbed one of each of the tourist brochures in the hotel's lobby. One in particular had a map of the town, which included a church called St. Andrews—evidently he was just as popular in Britain as he was in Scotland—which just happened to have two monuments on the premises called Giant's Grave and Giant's Thumb. It seemed like as good a place as any to start our investigation.

The church itself now loomed in front of us. It had been built from red stone, and its centerpiece was a tall crenellated tower that featured a large clock. A glance at my watch told me the clock was running two minutes fast.

"This is a lot bigger than the church Rob served at in Aberfoyle," I said, recalling the tiny ruined building Rina had dragged me to all those months ago. "Have you ever been here before?"

Anya shook her head. "I haven't. The English aren't very welcoming to my kind. I stay north of the border as much as possible."

I stopped walking and looked at her. "Are you all right with being here, now?"

"It's my fault Mum has laid this task on your shoulders. I need to help where I can."

I almost asked her if that was the only reason she was helping me, but I didn't. All the storybooks mention how fairies can't lie, and while I didn't know if that was a fact, I didn't want to risk it just then.

"The locals aren't welcoming to just giants, or all kinds of fairies?" I asked.

Anya shrugged. "In my experience, the English only care for the English. Here's the entrance."

The churchyard's gate was two stone pillars topped by gas lanterns, and an arch of black wrought iron connected the two overhead. A stone path led directly to the church's entrance at the base of the tower. We stepped through the gate and followed the flagstone path around the side of the church and to the graveyard. The grass was thick and lush, probably because of the never-ending fog that blanketed the area. The gravestones all looked to be a few centuries old, weather-stained and spotted with moss despite the obvious care the groundkeepers took with the area. Even though we were surrounded by ancient graves, it was quite obvious which stones we were looking for.

The Giant's Grave was a group of four low and wide stones—the brochure referred to them hogback stones—with a tall pillar set on either side. The hogback stones were intricately carved sculptures decorated with spirals and fluting, and what looked to me like runes.

"This is it," I said as we stood before the stones. "The brochure claims a Danish family is buried here."

"Perhaps a Dane or two was laid to rest here, in the beginning." Anya placed her palm on the closest hogback stone, and closed her eyes. "Since then, others have been imprisoned in these stones."

"How many are there?" I asked.

"No way to really tell without freeing them," she replied. "If I had to wager, I'd say one per stone, but in times past, whole families were crushed into a single one."

The back of my throat tightened; I'd never considered that giants had families. "Did the English hunt giants often?"

"They tried." She opened her eyes and glanced at the map. "The Thumb should be over this way."

Anya strode across the churchyard toward the Giant's Thumb, which was a six foot tall stone Celtic cross with the usual circular motif at the top. The monument was weather-beaten to the point that the top half of the cross had long since eroded away, and the lower portion wasn't faring much better.

"Interesting," I said as I read over the brochure. "This cross is the same age as many other Celtic crosses in the area, even in this very graveyard, but it's much more damaged. I wonder why?" I suspected the unusual weathering had to do with it being made from a softer stone than others; evidently Rina's geologist tendencies were rubbing off on me. Anya had a different theory.

"This stone is what's keeping the others imprisoned." She gingerly touched the Giant's Thumb with her fingertips, then turned her gaze back toward the hogback stones. "That's it, then. The magic held within this stone is so powerful that the cross itself is crumbling to dust. They will only be prisoners so long as this stone does not fail."

"Is it also keeping Meg imprisoned?" I asked.

"No. She's too far away for this magic to affect her." Anya placed both of her hands flat on the stone. "But it feels like the same wizard cast this spell. Was your uncle a giant hater?"

"First of all, we don't know if my uncle really did this," I began. "Second, if it was Uncle John then I doubt any of this was personal on his part. He's always been one to do anything for money."

"Ah. A wizard for hire, then." She straightened and dusted off her hands. "We've learned all we can here. Let's return to the room you rented and determine what's to be done about this mess."

Anya and I walked back to the hotel. By the time we arrived, the foggy drizzle had soaked through my coat and shoes, leaving me a damp, shivering mess. I was glad we'd agreed to leave exploring the giants' caves for another day.

The hotel room itself was something out of a bad sitcom. When we'd checked in, the front desk clerk had taken one look at Anya and me and decided we were on a romantic getaway, and had put us in Penrith's version of the honeymoon suite. The bed was enormous, and it was dressed in red and pink and topped with a tufted velvet head-board. Almost all of the furniture in the room was upholstered with red velvet, the woodwork had been painted gold, and the walls were adorned with copies of Renaissance paintings of Cupid and Psyche. I'd expected the tub in the *en suite* bathroom to be heart shaped, but it was a standard white porcelain model.

Anya loved the room. From the moment we set foot in it, she commented on how beautiful she found the artwork and the lush bedclothes. Normally I would have enjoyed the over the top décor too, but all the hearts and softness just made my heart ache.

"I'm going to take a shower," I announced, once we were in the room. I found the room service menu and handed it to Anya. "Could you please order us something to eat?"

I didn't wait for her to reply; her shocked face as I handed her the menu was more than enough. What, did she think I was going to ask her to shower with me, after she'd not only let her mother rip me up one side and down the other, and then disappear with no word if I'd ever see her again? No. There would be no shared showers, not today.

God, I missed the smell of her skin.

After I'd toweled off and dressed—in the bathroom, by myself—I emerged and saw Anya sitting on the bed with her back to me.

"Did you order?" I asked.

"Yes," she snapped. Since I didn't want to start an argument, I sat at the desk and opened my laptop. I'd just connected to the hotel's Wi-Fi when our dinner arrived. Anya opened the door and a far too cheery man pushed a cart into the room.

"Evenin' ma'am, and here's dinner for the two o' you," he said. He pushed the cart to the middle of the room and removed the shiny metal cloches with a flourish. "Now sir, here's your plate of sausages and chops."

"That one is mine," Anya said. "The salad is for him."

"A lass who likes her meat. Too few of them these days, in my opinion." He apparently wasn't impressed with my salad. When he finished arranging the plates and silverware on the side table, then he produced a few bottles of wine from underneath the cart.

"Now I realize you did not request wine, Mrs. Stewart, but I thought I'd best bring a selection," he said. I felt my jaw tense when he referred to Anya as Mrs. Stewart. If she was affected by that title in any way, she hid it well. "Fancy a glass or two? Or I can bring up a few beers, or anything else you'd prefer."

Anya opened her mouth, but I spoke first. "We'll take the red. Can you leave the bottle?"

"I surely can."

He uncorked the bottle and filled the glasses while I rooted in my wallet for tip money, but everything I had on me was American. As I was about to ask him if he'd be all right with me charging a tip to the room, Anya touched my elbow.

"I will take care of it," she said, then she signed the check for our meal and deftly handed over some money. I suppose being the daughter of a scary goddess slash barmaid teaches one how to tip well.

"Thank you," I said once we were alone again. "You didn't have to do that."

"I am aware of that." Anya sat and unfolded her napkin onto her lap. "Come and eat before the food gets cold."

I looked down at the salad she'd ordered for me. It was a standard garden salad, without grilled chicken or even cheese. We were having the most passive aggressive evening in history. "My food is already cold."

Anya took a bite of steaming hot sausage and smiled. I shook my head and speared a forkful of leaves. At least my dinner was healthy.

ASH AND JUNIPER

"You have got to be kidding me," I said.

"The Good People do enjoy a prank now and then," Robert said.

I shook my head. "This is more than a prank. This is downright evil."

It was eight o'clock on the nose, and Robert and I were at the address listed on my uncle's card, dressed and ready to join him for dinner. The property itself was beautiful. The centerpiece was a huge stone manor, maybe more than a century old. It was three stories tall, and I counted twenty windows across the front, which meant there were a lot of rooms in there. The grounds were well-maintained, with a neatly trimmed lawn bisected by a flagstone path that led to a grand entrance flanked by apple trees.

How did I know those were apple trees, even though there were no leaves or fruit present this early in the season? Because this house was the exact same house Robert and I had tracked my brother and the Seelie Queen to not six months ago.

"Why does my uncle live in a portal to Elphame?" I asked, remembering how we'd followed Chris and Nicnevin through the manor's front door and fell through time and space, and landed in Elphame on the road to the Seelie Court. "I don't want to go back there. Ever."

"Nor do I, but as ye so recently reminded me, ye are in truth a walker," Robert said. "If a portal scoops us up, ye can surely bring us home again."

I liked Robert's confidence. I liked it even more that he was confident in me.

"Well, then." I laced my fingers with his and squared my shoulders. "Let's go inside, and see what's for dinner."

Robert grinned, then we walked down the curved path toward the front steps and twin wooden doors. Each door had a tree carved into it, with the left being a stately broadleaf tree, and the right door bearing an evergreen.

"I don't remember these carvings," I said. "Maybe John remodeled after he moved in?"

"Ash and juniper," Robert said, nodding toward the doors. "Those trees are sworn enemies of one another."

I stopped moving. "What?"

"'Tis an Icelandic fable," Robert continued. "They say if an ash is planted on one side o' a home, and juniper along the other, the opposing forces will tear the home in twain."

"Is that some kind of an allegory for creating a portal?"

Robert reached out and traced the carvings. "Perhaps it is."

"I doubt it's just an interesting design choice." I took a deep breath and knocked on the door. It was opened by a woman wearing an actual maid's uniform, complete with a lace trimmed apron and little hat. I'd never seen anyone dressed this way, except at drunken costume parties.

"Hello," I said. "Karina Stewart and Robert Kirk, reporting for dinner."

She didn't bat an eyelash. "Right this way, if you please."

The humorless maid led Robert and me down a very long, very cold corridor that had a white and gray marble floor, and walls that were painted black above a white and gilt chair rail. The ceilings were sky high, and gold framed mirrors the size of elephants hung on the walls at regular intervals. But there weren't any portals to mystery dimensions in that hallway, at least none that I could detect, so that was something.

I also didn't see any regular doors along the corridor until we reached a large arch at its terminus. The maid gestured for Robert and me to enter, and we found ourselves in a dining room of a size and opulence to match the corridor. It was a rectangular room with vaulted ceilings decorated with even more gilding on the wooden support beams, while the area in between the beams was painted like the night sky. The walls were hung with large, colorful tapestries edged with gold braid and tassels. The dining table ran the length of the room and was covered in dark blue damask, along with an entire outlet mall's worth of cut crystal glassware and silver serving pieces.

"It looks like Uncle John has done well for himself," I said.

"Aye," Robert said. "Nicnevin herself rarely displays such wealth. If I didn't ken better, I'd say we were at a feast for kings."

Uncle John entered through a hidden door on the far end of the room, and smiled when he saw us. "Karina! Robert," he greeted. "I'm so glad you've come. Please, sit. Would you like some wine?"

"Just water for me," I said. John sat at the head of the table, and Robert at his left. I sat next to Robert; if John thought it odd that I kept Robert between us, he didn't mention it.

"As you wish." John nodded to the maid, and she poured glasses of wine for him and Robert. A second servant in an identical maid's costume set a glass of water next to my plate. "We'll be having roast beef tonight. I do hope you'll enjoy it."

"I'm sure we will," Robert said. A third servant—how many people did he employ?—pushed a cart toward the table. She set a basket of rolls on the table, and bowls of soup in front of us. It was a thick cream based soup, and while I might have enjoyed it a few months ago, recent experience had taught me that Faith wouldn't be a fan.

"It's nice that you live right here in Crail. What do you do for work?" I asked as I swirled my spoon in the soup. Robert grabbed a roll and set it next to my bowl.

"Oh, this and that," John replied. "Are ye in school still?"

"I'm almost done with my PhD in Geology," I replied, ignoring his deflection. For now. "I also minored in theoretical alchemy."

"Alchemy!" John clapped his hands together. "I'm an alchemist, have been for ages now. Must run in the family, eh?"

"Is that why you're keeping company at the Seelie Court?" Robert asked. "Does the queen have need of an alchemist?"

"I've no idea what Nicnevin's wants and needs are, nor how she fulfills them," John replied. "What made ye ask me about that?"

"We saw you at Doon Hill," I replied.

"Ah. Interesting, that ye returned to that spot," John said with a nod toward Robert.

"Why is that interesting?" Robert asked. "Since ye ken who I am, surely ye are aware that I am from Aberfoyle. What man does no' check in on his home when he is near?"

"Me, for one," John muttered. I thought his response was odd, but I filed it away for later.

"So what's happening up there on the hill?" I asked. "There were an awful lot of fairies milling about."

"That's all thanks to you, my dear," John replied. "Ever since you left the door within the Minister's Pine open, we've had a new way to leave Elphame without obtaining prior approval from the higher-ups, if you catch my meaning."

"The Good People couldn't travel between worlds before?" I asked.

"Surely they could, but before they needed a reason to be about," John replied. "Now there's a new unguarded avenue for all to traverse."

"Is that true? You needed approval to come here?" I asked Robert, but he only shrugged.

"I only went where herself sent me," he said.

"Always the good subject, ye were. Rumor has it that Nicnevin's still a bit sore o'er losin' ye." John signaled to the maids, and they removed our soup bowls and topped off his wineglass. "But now we can come here without task or mission, and enjoy ourselves away from their watchful gazes."

"So that's why Beira's mad," I deduced. "All these fairies are coming over with literally no reason to be here."

John's eyes narrowed. "Friends with Beira, are ye?"

"We've shared a pint or two," I replied.

"Why are there so few fae on the hill?" Robert asked. "There are hundreds if no' thousands o' creatures who'd give their eyeteeth to be out from under Seelie rule. When we were on the hill, I counted barely more than a hundred."

"Ah, well." John dropped his gaze to the table, and straightened his silverware. "The door, ye see, 'tis only open a wee bit. At first, only the little ones, sprites and the like, could wiggle through. O'er time it has widened a bit more, but not by much." John fixed me in his gaze. "If a walker were to permanently open the door, throw it wide as it were, now she could be quite well compensated for such an act."

A montage of the short time I'd spent in Nicnevin's castle played behind my eyes. "I don't think that's a good idea. Wouldn't people notice all the odd creatures flowing into this reality?"

"Most can no' see them." John leaned toward me, and asked, "How is it that you can see them, Karina?"

"Magic," I deadpanned.

John stared at me for another moment, then he smiled. "Aye, the magic is what first caught me eye as well. Perhaps you and I are more alike than we ever realized."

"I-I guess."

"Truth be told, I'd always assumed Christopher would be the next walker," John continued. "'Tis why I've kept up on him and his habits, since these traits are usually passed to the firstborn. But as he and I have never gotten on, I am certainly glad that the latest walker is you, Karina dear."

"You kept tabs on Chris?" I asked.

"I surely did," he replied. "You, as well."

"Did you tell Nicnevin that Chris might be a walker?"

John smiled, all teeth. "Now why would I go an' do that?"

I caught a whiff of the roast beef John's legion of servants was preparing, and I had a vision of eating his food and being trapped in that room for eternity.

"I'm sorry," I said. "I'm suddenly not feeling well. Jet lag, probably. Would it be all right if we rescheduled?"

"O' course." John rose and walked around toward my chair. Robert was on his feet in an instant and pulled out my chair before John reached me. "Let me see you two to the door."

"Thank you." I put my hand on Robert's elbow, and we followed John down the corridor of mirrors.

"Karina, would it be all right if I called on ye in a day or two?" John asked.

"I suppose," I replied. It's not like I had to answer the door. "Thank you for inviting us over tonight."

"Ye will always be welcome in my home, Karina."

Robert nodded at John, then we pushed open the oak doors and walked down the flagstone path. Neither of us looked back, not even once.

"Karina love," Robert said once we were on the main street and John's house was out of sight. "There is something amiss with that man."

"Yeah." I shivered. "I don't think we should go over there again."

"Wise choice. If ye are hungry, Beira's pub is a block east."

I smiled at my gallowglass. "Sounds like a plan."

Even though it was run by the Queen of Winter, Beira's pub was one of the warmest and most welcoming establishments I'd ever been in. The booths were upholstered in rich brown leather, and the tables and stools were dark, well-oiled wood. The lights were kept suitably low, and a fire crackled away in the hearth. All I needed was a blanket and mug of cocoa, and I could have stayed there forever.

The pub wasn't crowded, and Robert and I easily found a booth near the bar. Beira spotted us right away and smiled.

"Do you think it's a little weird for us to be here while she's mad at Chris?" I asked.

"Perhaps, but I would no' wish to offend her further by no' stopping in to say hello," Robert replied. "Courtesy means much to the old ones."

"I guess," I muttered. Before I could say anything further, Beira was standing at our table with two glasses of water and a menu.

"Welcome, welcome," Beira said as she set down the glasses. "It is indeed wonderful to have ye both back home where ye belong."

"It's great to be back," I said, and Robert agreed.

"Anya tells me that congratulations are in order," Beira continued. "Will the bairn arrive by next autumn?"

"Yes," I replied. "She'll be here at the end of summer."

"Ye are havin' lass, then. I shall craft her the most wonderful ice castle, and a wee crown o' snowflakes for her brow. Of course, she won't be able to play princess for a year or two, but we'll get her set up properly. I do love building palaces."

We all laughed, and I marveled at how Beira was acting completely different with us than how Chris had described her. "That will be awesome."

"Now then, are ye here for a bite?"

"Yeah. Our dinner plans didn't pan out." I studied Beira's face for a moment, then I continued, "As it turned out, my uncle has a house here in Crail. He invited us over for dinner, but we left without eating."

"Ah." Beira's long white fingers tapped the table. "Is this the uncle I am thinkin' of?"

"We believe so, yes," Robert said.

"Best stay away from that one," she said. "Hold fast, loves. I'll see what the kitchen has to offer ye."

With that the Queen of Winter disappeared into the pub's kitchen. I stared after her, then I turned to Robert with my mouth open, but he held up his hand.

"No' here," he warned.

I frowned, but held my words. I didn't like being told to be quiet, but he was right. The last thing we needed was for Beira to overhear us discussing her behavior.

The kitchen turned out to be on our side, and a few minutes after she'd disappeared into its depths Beira delivered a burger with a side of French fries to Robert, and a veggie platter for me. My platter was amazing, and in addition to the vegetables, it included bread, sliced cheeses, and a little cup of marinated olives.

"Thank you," I said as I tried not to dive into the olives. It was hard to remember your manners when you were starving. "This is perfect."

"I could no' stomach meat while I was with child, no' with any o' mine." Beira stroked my hair. "But the greens and cheeses will do ye bairn well. Eat up, love."

"Thank you," I said again. I watched Beira return to her post behind the bar, then I whispered, "Should we eat this?"

"Hm?" Robert grunted around a mouthful of food. He swallowed, and said, "'Twould be rude not to."

I popped an olive in my mouth. "Wouldn't want to be rude."

CHEESY HOTEL BED

T his cheesy, velvet-wrapped hotel bed was the most comfortable bed in the world. The universe, even. Best bed in the history of beds. It was firm yet soft, warm but not too warm, and the sheets smelled amazing. I was in heaven. Then I rolled over and nearly choked to death.

I sat up, spluttering and coughing as I unwound myself from the long strands of Anya's hair. Because Anya was in bed beside me. Holy hell, how had that happened?

Since she was still sleeping, I leaned back against the headboard, and tried to reconstruct the chain of events that had led to us being in bed together. I remembered us eating dinner; she'd even taken pity on my sad salad and offered me one of her chops. When we had finished the wine, we called down to the bar for a second bottle, and then...

Well, that was all I had. We were both fully dressed, so I imagined we'd gotten drunk and had decided to sleep it off. Then I spied the second bottle of wine, sitting on the table unopened.

Did she drug me? As soon as the thought formed in my mind, I knew it was foolish. Anya had no reason to drug me, certainly not so she could sleep next to me. Being that she was at least ten times stronger than I was meant that she could have thrown me into bed and held me there until I passed out without even breaking a sweat. The likely explanation was that I'd just fallen asleep after a day that began with a long drive and hours of walking, and ended with a meal and wine. Still, I wondered why she'd stayed, especially after how I'd been treating her.

I had every right to be mad at her, and she knew it. But I'd been punishing her ever since that afternoon in the pub, when in reality I was more mad at myself for letting Beira treat me like a dog. Beira's rant couldn't have been easy for Anya to hear, just like it couldn't have been easy for her to show up at the cottage after I'd been out all night. I hadn't even told her where I'd gone; for all she knew, I'd been sleeping with someone else. Despite me behaving like an ass for the last two days, Anya had stayed here and taken care of me.

I caressed Anya's cheek and tucked a stray piece of hair behind her ear. I do not deserve this woman.

I got out of bed and used the bathroom. Afterward, I checked the time; it wasn't yet four. On the way back to bed I shed my jeans, socks, and sweater, then I slid under the blanket and pulled Anya into my arms, pressing my face against her soft, impossibly flower-scented hair.

"Christopher," Anya mumbled. "What time is it?"

"It's early," I said. "Let's stay in bed a little longer."

"All right."

"Why'd you stay?"

"I wanted to." She rolled over and studied my face, her pupil-less eyes boring into mine. "Do you want me to leave?"

"No." I kissed her, and finally admitted to myself how I feared I might never kiss her again. "Never."

Anya slid her hands under my tee shirt and pushed it up toward my shoulders. I got up on my knees and pulled the shirt up and over my head. My mouth was on her neck before the garment hit the floor.

She was still wearing her pretty flowered dress, and as nice as it was, I wanted it gone. I plucked the buttons open one by one until I reached her waist. I slipped my hand against the bare skin of her side and she giggled; she was ticklish there. Anya's laughing intensified, then she hooked her leg around my hips and flipped us so I was on my back and she was straddling my waist.

"Promise me you'll never shut me out again," she said as she slid her arms free from her dress. She wasn't wearing much underneath it. In another moment, she wasn't wearing anything.

"I will, if you promise to never disappear on me again."

"Promise."

Anya lowered herself onto me. My back arched, and I squeezed her thigh, then she flung herself forward so her hair fell around my head. I loved how wild she was in bed, how she loved life... I loved her, and I would do anything to stay with her.

DON'T BORROW
PROBLEMS FROM THE
FUTURE

The morning after our impromptu pub dinner, I woke up alone in bed. Again. As my eyes welled up with pregnancy hormone-induced tears, I heard movement in the front of the cottage. There were lots of unfamiliar voices barking orders and directions, and much stomping about in what sounded like work boots.

Since my curiosity was stronger than my hormones, at least in this first trimester, I dressed myself in my loosest jeans and sweater and ventured forth. I found Robert standing next to the kitchen table, overseeing two men hauling in shipping crates and stacking them in the center of the common room.

"Karina me love," Robert said when he saw me. "I have made ye the coffee."

He presented me with a steaming mug of coffee. While I appreciated the gesture—and definitely needed the caffeine—the coffee was a secondary concern. "What's all this?" I asked.

"Our possessions have been delivered," he replied. I looked toward the open front door and saw the delivery truck parked in front of the cottage, and many of the boxes we'd had shipped overseas being unloaded and brought inside.

"So you got up when the delivery people knocked on the door?" I asked.

"I awoke long afore they arrived," he replied.

"Oh."

I sipped my coffee and watched the contractors haul in boxes labeled for Chris's room, the kitchen, and so forth; Chris's furniture was being held at their facility, which was great since we didn't have room for a second couch or third bed. The delivery guys and gals worked quickly and efficiently, just like the website had promised. If only getting my money's worth was my most important issue of the day.

Once all of the crates had been unpacked and brought inside, and I'd signed off on the receipts, the delivery guys went on their way. I decided that was as good a time as any to confront Robert. "Why won't you touch me anymore?"

He had the decency to look surprised. "I touch ye all the time."

"You know what I mean." I stomped across the room toward the kitchen, and yanked the fridge door open. Since we still hadn't gone grocery shopping, it was still empty. "We haven't had sex in weeks."

Robert stood behind me and set his hands on my shoulders. "Ye ken I do no' care for that clinical term."

"Fine. We haven't made love. Snuggled. Done it." I shut the fridge and faced Robert. "Is it me?"

"Why would ye think that?" Robert countered. "Karina, I've been wantin' ye since the day we met."

"Then why won't you do more than hold me?"

Robert pursed his lips, then he gathered me against his chest and tucked my head underneath his chin. It was his go-to move for calming me down, and the most infuriating part was that it worked every time. "I do no' want to hurt our bairn."

"How could us making love hurt the baby?" I leaned back and looked up at him. His brows were pinched together, his mouth pressed into a thin line. "Pregnant women can have sex right up until delivery. It won't hurt me, or Faith."

When I said our baby's name Robert's face lightened a bit. "Have I told ye how much I love that ye named her afore she ever was? Truly, she will be the most adored child that e'er lived." He exhaled a great breath and tucked a lock of hair behind my ear. "Ye have heard me speak o' me past wives."

Not my favorite subject, but I had started this discussion. "I have."

"After me first wife bore our son, she never quite recovered. She died while he was still a wee thing. Years later, I married Margaret, but the Good People took me before she bore our child. I never once got to hold him."

"I'm sorry. That's... that's awful." My thoughts raced inside my mind. What if something did happen to me, and I never got to meet Faith? What if something happened to Robert? What if—

I squeezed my eyes shut and took a breath, then another. I refused to let Robert's anxiety fuel my own worries. Once I'd calmed myself down, I put my hands on the sides of his head and forced him to look me in the eyes. "You know that neither of those things will happen now, right? Faith isn't in any danger, medical or magical."

"No. I don't." Robert broke away from me and paced across the kitchen. "All I ken is that the same misfortune never visits twice. For all I ken this time around you'll be carried off by the Good People instead o' me."

"If that happens I'll just walk back home. I'm a walker, remember? They can't trap me in Elphame."

"As if that were the whole o' it."

"Then tell me the rest." When he remained silent, I continued, "I thought we were in this together. Partners."

"We are."

"Then talk to me. Tell me what's wrong." I tried smiling, but I felt more like bawling. "I can't fix things unless you tell me what's broken."

"Can ye fix me, then? Can ye reach inside me muddled old brain and stop me worries, and convince me that I can keep ye safe?" He turned around and stared out the window into the garden, his hands braced on the edge of the kitchen sink. I stood behind him and slid my arms around his waist, and rested my cheek against his back.

"Who can keep us safer than you? I don't think anyone would dare harm the gallowglass's bride. Or his child."

"There are monsters in this world and the next that would hurt ye just for the sake o' hearin' ye scream."

"But we aren't like most mortals. We can see the monsters, and we can outsmart them. We've done it before, a bunch of times."

"But—"

"But nothing." We stood there for a moment, me listening to his heartbeat. "You know what you're doing? You're borrowing problems from the future."

He looked back over his shoulder. "What's that, now?"

"My mom had pretty bad anxiety. She used to get worked up over all sorts of things, but the worst was when she worried about things that hadn't even happened yet. Whenever she did that, Dad said she was borrowing problems from the future, and maybe she should put those problems back where they belong."

Robert grunted. "I would if I could."

"I know it's easier said than done. I know you can't just shut off the worry, like a faucet. But maybe, when you worry, you could talk to me, and maybe we can work on those things together."

Robert grasped my hand and squeezed. "A sound plan. Ye are brilliant, Karina me love."

"You know it." I stepped back and glanced out the window. It was a beautiful sunny day, and I refused to waste it. "Come on. Let's take a walk."

The frown returned. "It's still early, and more than a bit damp. Will ye be warm enough?"

"I'll wear gloves, and a scarf. Besides," I continued as I put on my jacket, "there's a medical center in town. I want to stop in and make an appointment."

"Appointment for what?" he demanded.

"Prenatal care has improved about a billion percent in the past few hundred years," I replied. "They can run tests on me, give me vitamins, and make sure Faith is the healthiest baby on the planet."

Robert nodded, but the creases on his forehead didn't ease up. "In my day, one only sought a doctor when things were no' goin' well."

"We're living in my day now, and it's called preventative care," I said. "So let's go, talk to a professional, and maybe that professional can reassure you enough to ease off some of those concerns."

Robert blew out a breath and grabbed his coat. "I agree on one condition. If this so-called professional gives ye a list o' recommendations while ye carry Faith—be it bed rest, giving up coffee, whatever it may be—you and I will follow it to the letter."

I halted, scarf in hand. "Coffee?"

"*Karina.*"

"Okay, okay. I agree."

"Aye, then." Robert opened the front door, then he pushed me aside and summoned his sword. "Who the bloody Christ are you?"

"I'm sorry, I thought Chris Stewart lived here," came a familiar voice. "Put down the sword, man. You treat all lost strangers this way?"

I peeked around Robert and saw Chris's best friend, Ethan, standing on the other side of the door. Ethan was as adorable as ever, all rumpled brown hair that matched his rumpled navy jacket and khaki pants. His arms were overflowing with books and loose papers, which would offer him little protection against Robert's claymore.

"Robert, this is Chris's friend, Ethan," I said as I gently pushed down his sword arm. "Let's not kill him, okay?"

Robert grunted and stepped aside. I turned to Ethan and smiled, hoping his long friendship with Chris meant he wouldn't call the police on us.

"It's great to see you," I said.

"You too, Rina." He shifted the weight of the books he was carrying. "Mind if I come in and set these down? I'm not as strong as I look."

"Of course." I led Ethan to the kitchen table and helped him unload the books and reams of notepaper. "We have fresh coffee, if you'd like some."

"Absolutely." Ethan took a seat while Robert poured the coffee. He set a mug in front of Ethan, then he took up a position against the kitchen counter.

"Thank you." Ethan glanced at Robert. "Are you going to introduce us?"

"Oh! Sorry! Ethan, this is Robert Kirk. We're sort of engaged."

Robert's eyes narrowed. "Sort of?"

"Well, we don't have a date or anything!"

Ethan rose and extended a hand to Robert. "Good to meet you," Ethan said, as they shook hands. "Chris has told me wonderful things about you. Didn't mention the sword, though."

"Christopher has spoken of ye as well," Robert said, and his shoulders relaxed a bit.

"Chris also said that you two were in a family way," Ethan added with a sly look. "Any truth to that rumor?"

"One hundred percent accurate," I replied. "Faith will be here in late September. Maybe early October."

Ethan grinned. "Congratulations, both of you."

"Thank you," I said. Robert smiled, and set about making himself a cup of tea. "Not that I'm not glad to see you, but why have you come by?"

"I'm sorry to just show up like this, but I've been trying to reach Chris. Is he around?"

"He went to Cumbria," I replied. "In England."

"That have anything to do with the girlfriend whose mother hates him?" Ethan asked.

"I wouldn't say Beira hates him," I replied. "It's more that she's a bit overprotective." Robert snorted. "Okay, maybe Chris isn't her favorite person."

"I gathered that when he came to visit me the other day." Ethan shuffled through his papers until he found a cocktail napkin covered in Chris's messy scrawl. "He asked me for help with some local folklore, specifically a wizard called Scot and a megalith called Long Meg and Her Daughters."

"That's why he went to England," I said. "He went down to have a look at the megalith. Why? Did you find something?"

"I believe I did." Ethan dug out one of his books, opened it to a marked section, and held it out to me. It was an illustration of a woman on one page, while the facing page was a large standing stone.

"That's Meg, both before and after running afoul of the wizard," Ethan said. "Anyway, Chris was interested in learning how to free Meg, which apparently can be done, but you can't approach it head on. That's probably going to be his biggest problem. You know how he tends to be bullheaded."

"Do I ever." I traced the outline of the stones. "So, how do we get her out? Knock three times?"

"If only." Ethan reached over and turned the page, revealing an illustration of the stone circle beyond Meg. "The key to freeing her is not with Meg, but the rest of the circle. The stones are enchanted, so you can never count them properly. In order to free Meg, you need to count them correctly twice in a row."

"And then she just pops out of the stone?" I read the caption below the illustration. "It says there are fifty-nine stones. Can't you just yell out fifty-nine two times, and be done with it?"

"Ye are forgettin' a key aspect o' these curses," Robert said. "If 'tis the stones that are spelled, like as no' they cannot easily be counted. Perhaps they move when ye aren't watchin', or perhaps a rise in the meadow obscures some, so ye' overlook them. Remember, the Good People do love their pranks."

"They do seem to be feisty little buggers," Ethan agreed.

I got up and found my laptop. "I'm going to email this information to Chris," I said as I set it on the coffee table. This seemed like too many details for a text message, and if I knew Chris, he'd already gotten up early to get in some writing before heading out into the real world. "Ethan, did you know that Robert attended St. Andrews?"

"Did you?" Ethan swiveled around in his chair and regarded Robert. "What year did you graduate?"

"Long before ye came on, that's for certain," Robert replied.

"Couldn't be that's many years before me," Ethan pressed.

Robert glanced at me. I nodded. Robert smiled, and said, "I graduated from St. Andrews in the year of Our Lord sixteen hundred and sixty-one."

Ethan's jaw dropped. "Robert, you'd better grab the Scotch from Chris's room," I said. "Ethan, we've got a hell of a story for you."

FOR SURE

I read and then re-read the email from Rina. It seemed that Ethan had come through for me yet again, and figured out exactly how we could set Meg free.

"Anya," I said over my shoulder. "Come see this."

She moved behind me, stooping to wrap her arms around my shoulders and nuzzle my ear. I loved that we were acting like lovers again. "A message from the sister, is it?"

"It is. It seems that we need to count the stones in the circle behind Meg and get the same number twice." I twisted around until I could see Anya's oil slick eyes. "How hard can that be?"

Three hours later, I had my answer. It was very, very hard.

"This place is cursed," I muttered. The first time we counted Meg's daughters there were fifty-nine of them, the exact same amount of stones that were mentioned in all the guidebooks and on the local tourist websites. The second time we counted the stones, there were fifty-eight.

The third time there were sixty stones.

And the fourth time we went 'round the circle, we counted seventy-three.

"It's not a curse, just the spell at play," Anya said. "The stones are probably rearranging themselves, so they can give us a bit of a challenge."

"Then how are we supposed to count them?" I whined. I, a grown, educated man, whined at my girlfriend whilst standing on a windswept moor. I could almost hear the Brontës' rolling over in their graves.

"Surely by now you understand that magic tends to have a sense of humor," Anya said. "What we need to do is outwit the spell."

"Outwit, huh?" I had wits. At one time in my life I would have described myself as intelligent, even. While I was no scientist like Rina, I could definitely figure out a thing or two.

"Okay. So." I completed a three hundred and sixty degree pivot, thus ensuring that all of the stones could be seen from the spot of ground I was standing on. The cows were out as well, but they were keeping to one side of the circle. I supposed that was good. "I have an idea, but I don't know how to pull it off."

"Tell me," Anya said. "Maybe I can help."

"What we need to do is keep all of the stones in our line of sight while we count them," I explained. "That way, they can't hide or move to another place in the circle. If, between you and me, we're able to keep our eyes on them, we can count them properly. Hopefully, we can do it twice." Why did they have to be counted twice? Oh, yeah. Because magic.

"I can make it so we have a right fine view of them," Anya said slowly, "but you must promise not to scream. Or faint."

I could not imagine why I'd do either, save for screaming at these mischievous rocks to stay put. "Okay. I promise."

Anya kissed me hard, then she walked about ten paces away from me. In the next moment she was twenty feet tall.

Twenty. Feet. Tall.

"You promised you wouldn't faint," Anya said, when I stumbled backward, staring up at her. Her voice had magnified along with her stature, and it boomed across the countryside. A few of the cows mooed in protest, then returned to grazing.

"I won't," I said. "Warn me next time, okay?"

She smiled, the biggest, toothiest smile in the history of smiles. "All right, then. Want to hop up for a look 'round?"

"Sure," I replied, and realized too late what she meant. Anya picked me up like a rag doll and deposited me on her shoulder. Good thing I've never been scared of heights or intimidated by tall women.

"How did your clothes get bigger?" I wondered.

She cleared her throat. "It's a glamour."

"Anya. Are you naked? Wait, have your clothes been glamours this whole time?"

"Hush. I need to concentrate."

"All right." I would definitely ask her about her potential nakedness later on. "Can you see all of them?" Anya moved, and I grabbed her hair to keep from sliding off her shoulder. "Slowly!"

"Sorry. Hang on, now?"

"I am hanging on," I said, then she grew even taller. "How big can you get?" I asked, as I looked down at the ground.

"Big enough." She rotated clockwise, giving us a look at each stone in turn. "Start counting, love."

I stood on her shoulder, grasping her hair as if it was a vine and I was Tarzan—actually, I was more like Jane in this scenario—and counted the stones out loud. After I reached the fifty-ninth stone, I started over. And got fifty-nine the second time.

"We did it," I said. "Let's see if she's out."

It only took Anya a few steps to cross the hundred or so yards to where Long Meg sat outside the stone circle. Once there, she returned to her usual size and jumped into my arms. "We did it together," she said.

"Yeah, we did."

I resisted the urge to kiss her, since if I was Meg the last thing I'd want to see when I was newly freed from hundreds of years in a stone prison would be two unfamiliar people making out in front of me. Not that Meg was loose.

"Where is she?" I wondered.

Anya stepped up to the stone and traced some of the spirals carved into the surface. "Meg? You can come out. It's safe now." When nothing happened, she added, "My mum sent me to free you. Beira, you remember her?"

The stone shuddered, and a woman who I assumed was Meg stepped out. She was rather tall but still human-sized at about six feet, and she had long dark hair and flashing green eyes. She was also completely naked.

"Beira, eh," Meg said, then she looked at me. "And what made ye come along? Are ye a wizard?"

"Beira said my uncle was responsible for putting you in stone," I replied. "She sent me to free you."

Meg leaned toward me and sniffed. I'd just been smelled by a giant-ess. "Ye are no' o' the Scot line."

"He changed his name to John Damian," I said. "He's still around."

Meg shook her head. "The man that imprisoned me has been dead for many centuries. Got conked in the head wi' a stone while he said his prayers, but do no' ask me how I came by that knowledge." Meg grinned, and I understood that even while she'd been trapped in the stone, she hadn't been helpless. I also wondered how Beira could have made such a gross mistake in the identity of Meg's imprisoner.

"Will the two o' ye be helpin' the rest, then?" Meg asked.

Anya and I looked at each other. "The rest?" I asked.

"Aye," Meg replied. "The rest o' the giants."

"Ah, then, here's how he did it," Meg said as she examined the carvings on the Giant's Thumb. During the drive and subsequent walk from the field where the stones sat to the town proper, Meg explained that Michael Scot had imprisoned several giants in the hogback stones at St. Andrews's graveyard; apparently, he'd done all of his giant hunting for cash and fame. Based on that description, I understood how people had confused the wizard of eight hundred years ago with my mon-ey-grubbing uncle here in the present day. What I didn't understand is how Beira had confused them, what with Scot being long dead and my uncle still very much alive.

More importantly, at least for the moment, was that Meg thought she knew how to break the spell and free the rest of the giants imprisoned in the graveyard. I had a few reservations over freeing them, since I didn't know why they're been imprisoned in the first place. Maybe they were giant criminals, who knew? But the prospect of freeing them made Anya happy, and since she was half giantess I went along with the plan. It's not as if I could have stopped her, or Meg, even if I'd wanted to.

Also of note was that Meg remained completely, unabashedly naked. I'd offered her my coat, the blanket folded up in the car's trunk, and to bring her to a shop to buy her a whole new set of clothes, and she'd politely declined each of my suggestions. She also refused to enact a glamour to make it appear as if she was clothed, much like how Anya had preserved her modesty earlier. According to Meg she'd been encased in stone for so long she wanted nothing but air and sunlight on her skin, and she assured me that mortals couldn't see her. When I'd pointed out that I was mortal and could see her just fine she'd ruffled my hair and said I was a special case.

Now I stood in a churchyard with two giantesses, one of them naked as a blue jay, and I wasn't feeling special at all. Foolish, perhaps, and in imminent danger of being arrested as an accessory to public indecency, but not special.

"See here," Meg said as she bent down and traced one of the worn engravings on the Giant's Thumb. "He looped and looped the spell in and around itself." She straightened and gazed toward the hogback stones. "We must untie the knot. That's how we'll get the rest loose."

"How do we do that?" I asked.

Meg glanced at me over her shoulder and grinned. "The two of ye are such a lovely pair, both with the yellow hair and wonderful big eyes. 'Tis no wonder ye love each other so."

All the blood rushed to my face, making me simultaneously hot and dizzy. "The knot?"

"Aye, the knot." Meg walked around the monument clockwise, then counterclockwise. "Feel that? We must turn it widdershins to undo what harm's been done."

"Widdershins?" I repeated as Anya grabbed my hand and pulled us into step behind Meg. We walked counterclockwise around the old stone cross, and walked, and walked.

"I'm going to wear through my shoes," I said after a small eternity of trudging.

"Then just take them off," Anya suggested.

"Take everything off and feel the crisp air and warm sun on ye as the gods intended," Meg added.

"Thanks. I'll be fine." Out of the corner of my eye, I spied movement near the hogback stones. The stones shuddered and tipped outward, and the ground around them heaved as if something was coming up. "I think this is working."

Meg went from six feet tall to fifty in the blink of an eye, leaned over for a closer look at the hogback stones, and was back to six feet again. It was enough to make my mortal stomach tie itself in a knot. "Aye, surely 'tis. Faster now! They're breaking loose!"

Sweat beaded my forehead as we jogged around the stone cross. I could hear discordant sounds emanating from the stones, reminiscent of piano strings snapping. As those snaps and wails increased in volume, the gravestones' movement went from shaking to a full on tremor. We were pulling the wizard's knot apart, string by string, and setting Meg's people free.

The ground shook so hard I stumbled, and grabbed onto the Giant's Thumb to steady myself. Across the churchyard, the four hogback stones gave one final heave and fell outward, flat on their sides. A hole had opened up in the center of the stones, and giant after giant emerged from the earth and into the sunlight.

"They're free," Anya said, her eyes shining. "After all this time. Mayhap we can free all of them, like the ones in the cave?"

"Someday we shall," Meg said, then she placed her hands on Anya's shoulder. "Ye have done a brave and wonderful thing, lass. Tell your Mum that old Meg owes a great boon to her, and to you and your lad. We all owe ye a great many things."

Anya smiled and ducked her head, then Meg left us and went to rejoin her people. I wrapped my arm around Anya's shoulders and we watched the newly-free giants as they climbed out of their prison.

"We did a good thing," I said. "I am proud of us."

"I am proud of you," Anya said. "And Mum will be too, I'm sure of it."

"And if she isn't?"

Anya laid her head on my shoulder. "If she isn't, then she'll just have to get over it. You're staying in my life no matter what she has to say about it, that's for sure."

I tightened my arm around her. "For sure."

ETHAN'S AN INSIGHTFUL ONE

"**G**iants are loose," I announced as I read a text from Chris. "In other news, Chris and Anya are back together."

"Are those both good things?" Ethan glanced toward Robert. "Especially the part about the giants."

"I guess we'll find out." I texted Chris a thumbs up emoji, then I set down my phone and rubbed my temples. At least one of our problems had been solved. As for the problem of the door I'd left open on Doon Hill, Robert, Ethan, and I had been discussing what to do about that for the better part of the day; that, and convincing Ethan that Robert was the gallowglass.

It wasn't that Ethan didn't believe us. He'd attended Carson University—the foremost magic school in the US—along with Chris, and understood that there was more in heaven and earth than could be explained by scientific means. However, he remained firm in his belief that magic was gone from the mortal realm, save for a few lingering pockets. Those lingering pockets were how he'd rationalized Robert's ability to summon his sword from thin air. In the end, he agreed to keep an open mind, and that was good enough for me.

"Maybe we can burn down the tree," I mused.

"And what if the fire spread down the hill and toward the village?" Robert countered. "What if it spread through the portal and into Elphame?" He shook his head. "While fire would be an effective end to the tree, there are too many unknowns for my liking."

"What if we spread a ring of salt around the tree?" I asked hopefully, then I realized something. "I guess that would only work until the rain washed it away."

"Or the wind blew it off," Robert added.

"Maybe we're approaching this all wrong," ever-practical Ethan said. "We're discussing this door as if it's something magical. What if it's really just a door?"

"It can't be just a door." I looked at Robert. "Can it?"

"I do no' see why not," Robert replied. "When we both went to Elphame to retrieve Christopher, we entered the portal through a quite ordinary door, and we came back out the same way."

"Huh." I leaned back in my chair. Of all the crazy questions I'd thrown at Robert, never once had I asked him what it was like inside the Minister's Pine. "What was it like when you were inside the tree?"

"Dark," Robert replied. "No' cold, but damp. Stale, like a room no living body had entered for quite some time."

"Like a closet?" I asked, and Robert nodded.

"Or the inside of Nicnevin's dark, dank heart," Ethan said.

"For someone who officially doesn't believe in fairies, you make a lot of insightful connections," I said.

"I am merely performing my duty as a scholar," he replied. "Robert, how did you end up getting loose from this tree?"

"Karina freed me," Robert replied.

"She did?" Ethan asked. "Will you tell me about it, both being in the tree and escaping it?"

"Do you remember much of it?" I asked as I leaned forward, eager to hear his answer.

"I remember everything," Robert began. "From the first time Nicnevin sent me there to the last, and every dark day in between. That collar she placed 'round me neck? Some days when I wake, I still feel it. I remember it all."

Ethan flipped to a blank page in his notebook. "You say it was dark? Was there any sound?"

"No sounds came from within, save for whate'er noise I made meself," Robert replied. "Scuffin' me feet and the like. The only other sounds were from outside the tree, birdsong and the rustling o' the trees. Occasionally a person happened by; sometimes, they would talk to the tree or leave a trinket. Usually they just went about their business, paying the tree no mind." Robert raised his head and speared me with his gaze. "And then there was the day ye came to the hill."

"Me?" I asked.

"What did Rina do?" Ethan asked, not looking up as he scribbled away. "Before she freed you, that is."

"First, she had a bit of a row with Christopher."

Ethan shook his head. "Sounds like our Chris."

"He was having a bad day," I added.

"After he left the clearing, Karina placed her hand on the tree and said that she believed in me." Robert reached across the table and took my hand. "Ye were no' the first—or even the hundredth—person I'd heard speak to or touch the tree, but when ye did it I felt the warmth o' ye. It was like ye were touchin' me instead o' the bark."

"I remember feeling like the tree had heard me," I said. "I guess that was you."

"Aye. 'Twas me."

"And how did you exit?" Ethan prompted.

"I heard Karina retreat down the trail and I stood there strainin' me ears to catch another snippet o' her voice. I remembered the last thing she'd said—"

"That I'd free you if I could," I said.

Robert tightened his fingers on mine. "Aye. And then there was a slice o' sunlight streamin' into the void I'd been trapped in, and I stepped out o' the tree and back into the world. That was the first time ye rescued me."

"You owe me what, three rescues now?" I teased. "Or are we up to four?"

"Four? Bah."

"So it is like a door," Ethan said. "Or at least a rudimentary point of egress. After your exit, did you look back at the tree? Do you remember seeing a crack in the trunk, or any other opening? Robert? Robert!"

"Oh, no, nothing like that." Robert winked at me as he squeezed my fingers, warming me right to my toes. "After I stepped out o' the pine, the tree was as solid as ever."

"I don't remember seeing any cracks in the tree either," I said. "Not when I went back and met Robert, or when we were there a few days ago."

"Perhaps the door is disguised." Ethan rubbed his chin. "Or perhaps it's an optical illusion, like that road in the Midwest where cars appear to roll uphill. Either way, I think what we need to do is treat this phenomenon as the door it is. We need to think about it as an actual door, rather than a metaphorical one."

"Makes sense," I said. "How do we think about doors?"

"How do doors become broken?" Ethan got up and approached the door to Chris's bedroom, his hand on his chin as he considered it. "In my day, I've dealt with loose jambs, squeaky hinges, and locks that acted against my best interests. Have you any tools we could use?"

"I've got tons of tools," I said, full of confidence as I stood and located the shipping crate that held my prospecting kits. "I've got pickaxes, a field and a lab microscope, tons of goggles, a few spades—"

"Woodworking tools," Ethan clarified.

"Oh." I sat on the couch. "Um, none of those. I work with rocks, not wood."

My phone sounded off. I grabbed it and saw number I didn't recognize, but it had a New York area code so I accepted the call. "Hello?"

"Hello. Is this Karina Stewart?"

"Yes. Who's calling?"

"This is Maisie Perkins. I'm your brother's agent. We met at the release party, remember?"

"Um, yeah. How can I help you?"

"Are you with Chris? He isn't answering his phone."

An image of Chris cavorting with giants played behind my eyes. Amazingly, I didn't laugh. "He's not here with me. Maybe you should send him a text."

Maisie huffed. "I have been texting him. And calling, and emailing. Can you get in touch with him?"

"I can, but maybe you should just be patient. He's a pretty busy guy. He'll respond to you when he has time."

"Karina, this is very important—"

"I'm sure it is. Have a great day!"

I ended the call, then I set my phone face down on the table.

"What was that about?" Robert asked.

"Just Chris's agent," I replied. "We were talking about tools?"

"As I was tellin' Ethan, I'm sure we can locate a few basic tools," Robert said. "A hammer and a plumb line should do to start."

"Was my reverend also a carpenter?"

"Your reverend was a poor man who repaired his home himself," Robert replied. "Feel up for a walk to the shops?"

Now that he mentioned it, I did feel a nap coming on. "What about Dougal's toolbox?" I asked. "It might have what we need."

Robert frowned. Hard. "I do no' think using anything more from him is in our best interests."

"But he said that we can use his truck, and his toolbox, whenever we need it," I said. "Is it so strange that he might have been sent to help us? Would that be stranger than the Cailleach Bheur sending my brother on a quest to free a giantess from a block of stone?"

"Ye have a point. But who would ha' sent MacKay here in the first place?"

I felt a hand on my arm, even though Robert and Ethan were on the other side of the room. I looked to my left and felt the blood drain from my face.

"I did," Nicnevin purred.

CARETAKING

"How the hell did you get in here?" I demanded as I scrambled to the far side of the couch. Robert was there, yanking me to my feet and pushing me behind him and away from the Seelie Queen.

"I have my ways," Nicnevin replied.

Just like the fairy queen of legend, Nicnevin was the most beautiful woman I'd ever seen, either in real life or in fashion magazines. She had long, wavy red hair, green eyes that slanted upward at the outer corners, and impossibly smooth alabaster skin. Today she was wearing a diaphanous green gown that did more to enhance her body than conceal it, a crown of white and pink hawthorn flowers, and gold shoes that sparkled more than any footwear had the right to.

Despite all of her beauty, Nicnevin was as wicked as they came. She was easily the most dangerous person I've ever encountered, and I've met Hades. And she was sitting on my couch.

"Robert, are you enjoying playing house with your little walker?" Nicnevin asked.

"You've no right to be here," Robert said. "We serve Fionnlagh, no' ye!"

"Does that mean you won't accept my gift?" she asked. "And who's this?" Nicnevin smiled at Ethan.

"What gift?" I asked. "You don't give things without strings attached."

"How would you know? I've never given you anything before." When no one responded, Nicnevin continued, "I suspected that you two might need help fixing what happened on Doon Hill, so I sent you my very best handyman. Hasn't he been a great help to you both?"

"You mean Dougal?" I asked.

"The walker comprehends." Nicnevin yawned, and stretched like a cat. "Then he has been helpful."

"I suppose." I looked up at Robert, who shook his head. "No, not really. He's the worst. Yeah, he's got to go."

"We can no' accept anything from ye, no' wi'out first speakin' wi' Fionnlagh," Robert said.

"I'm here."

Robert and I turned as one, and saw Fionnlagh, the Seelie King and Nicvenin's husband, leaning against the kitchen counter. Ethan gaped from the Seelie King to the Queen, his eyes and mouth as wide open as they could get.

"My lord," Robert said with a shallow bow. "Is MacKay truly here to help us?"

"I understand you're both suspicious, and rightly so, of a gift from Nicnevin," Fionnlagh began, "but Dougal's sole purpose on this plane is to assist you assimilate back to your lives in Scotland. He has the full backing of the Seelie Court."

Which meant that he wasn't just sent by Nicnevin, but Fionnlagh too. "Why did you think we needed help?" I asked. "Is Doon Hill really that bad?"

"If you don't mind my subjects winnowing away and important tasks in Elphame going undone, no, it's not bad at all," Nicnevin said. "If you mind the effect of thousands of unbridled fae roaming unchecked amidst unknowing mortals, then this is quite a predicament."

"You care about what happens to mortals?" I asked.

"Of course we do," she replied. "Why would we let this tide flow unchecked? Do you think the mortal world would survive as it is with a fairy court growing in its midst?"

"That's what they're doing, then," Robert said. "Those who ha' come o'er wish to live without governance like the Wild Fae of old."

"And I'm sure you remember how well that went," Nicnevin said. "Mortals and magic don't mix well together."

"Maybe that's why magic's gone from this world," I said. Fionnlagh looked at me and smiled.

"Astute deduction, walker," he said.

I returned his smile, but I didn't thank him. I knew better than to go around uttering thanks when Nicnevin was in earshot.

"There is a second reason we sent Dougal," Fionnlagh continued. "You were both treated rather unfairly by the Olympian gods. We hoped that by easing your transition back to Scotland, you might be inclined to remain."

There it was: the Seelie Court wanted Robert and me to be their permanent subjects and were willing to bribe us to keep us happy. Lucky for them, my crazy mentor had soured us for living in the states, at least for the time being.

"Perhaps we shall remain. 'Tis a fine cottage, after all," Robert said. He usually thanked Fionnlagh when appropriate, but Nicnevin was in the room. The last thing we needed was to word something incorrectly around her and end up as her slaves for the next thousand years.

"That would please us." Fionnlagh strode toward Nicnevin and extended his hand. She accepted it and stood, all the while smiling at her husband. "Both of us."

"Be kind to Dougal," Nicnevin said, never taking her gaze from Fionnlagh. "He has been instructed to assist you whenever necessary. And if he fails, we'll kill him."

"What?" I demanded, forgetting that one shouldn't really shout at royalty, especially magically powered royalty.

Nicnevin peeked around Fionnlagh's shoulder and smiled at me. "Or perhaps we'll turn him into a toad. We like toads."

With that, the two faded from view. I blew out a relieved breath and leaned against Robert. "Do they really turn people into toads?"

Robert shrugged. "Verra little from those two would surprise me."

"I bet."

"Were they really fairies?" Ethan asked. I'd forgotten all about him. "Did they really just appear and vanish, like poof?"

"Welcome to our magical life," I said. "Were they your first?"

"That's a rather personal question, don't you think?" Ethan downed what was left of his coffee. "Maybe I should have taken you up on that Scotch."

"Are you okay?" I asked. "Thinking about magic is one thing, but seeing it can really tie your brain up in knots."

"I can handle it. At least, I think I can." Ethan gathered up his notes and stacked them on top of his books. "Besides, I'd best be getting back to university. I have a class early tomorrow."

"Okay. Thank you for helping us," I said. "Call me if you need to talk about... any of this." Robert shook Ethan's hand and thanked him as well.

"Of course," Ethan said. "And don't be afraid to shout if you need me. I'm always willing to help you and your foolish brother."

After Ethan left, I faced Robert. "How could Ethan see them without the fairy ointment?"

"As I said, verra little about those two would surprise me." Robert looked toward the truck's key hanging on the peg. "I assume ye now wish to examine the toolbox."

"I think that would be best."

Robert blew out a breath. "I fear you're correct. I'll fetch it."

I sat at the kitchen table, looking over the notes Ethan had left for us while Robert went out to the truck and retrieved the tool box. When he reentered the cottage, he set the shiny red box on the floor in the center of the common area and opened the top. The tool box unfolded from the center, revealing a detachable tray on either side. Robert removed that tray, and the next. And the next.

"I guess anything we need really is in there," I said. Robert had taken seven trays out of the toolbox, even though the box looked like it could only hold two or three. "Are there any carpentry tools?"

"I've found a square, and a few hammers," Robert replied. He peered into the box, squinting toward the bottom. "Karina, you'd best have a look at this."

"Okay."

I stood up, and my vision swam. My knees turned to water, and I went down. My elbows caught the edge of the table before I hit the floor. I panted, furiously blinking at the spots swirling in front of my eyes. Then everything went dark.

When I came to, I was lying on the couch, the top half of me cocooned in Robert's arms and a blanket covering my legs. It was way too warm and claustrophobic, but when I tried stretching, Robert tightened his hold on me. His forehead was pressed against the top of my head, his breathing shallow and ragged. Robert was scared.

"Did I pass out?" I asked.

"Aye. Ye stood up and went down straight away. I almost didn't catch ye."

"Good thing I'm short, so I didn't have far to go."

"Karina."

His voice caught on my name. I wiggled around in his arms until my cheek was against his chest and my hand over his heart.

"I'm sorry. But I'm okay, really. I just got a little dizzy."

"When did ye last eat?"

"Um. Breakfast?"

"That was hours ago. Ye need to eat more often."

"I'm not even hungry."

"Ye're so no' hungry ye fainted. What if I had no' been here? What if ye fell and hit your head, what then?"

"I don't need a babysitter, or someone to tell me when to eat. I've been taking care of myself since my parents died over ten years ago, pretty well I might add."

"Ye no longer have just yourself to care for."

I didn't have anything to say to that, since he was right. Robert tilted my chin toward him. "Love, I ken that ye are strong. Truly, ye are the strongest person I have e'er met, but ye need to let me take care o' ye, at least for now."

I wanted to argue, tell him that I knew what was best for me and the baby, cite the numerous books and articles I'd read on pregnancy and parenting... But I didn't do any of those things. I couldn't, not while Robert was gazing at me with his eyes filled with concern and fear, and love.

"All right, Dr. Kirk." I sat up a bit straighter and wound my arms around his neck. "What are your orders?"

He grinned, though a bit of concern remained in his eyes. I supposed that was all right. "Firstly, ye will eat when I tell ye to. If ye aren't hungry, just a bite or two will do. Broth is good for women wi' child, and bread. Soon enough ye'll be so hungry ye may eat us out o' house and home."

I giggled. "I can't wait to want bacon again."

"And I can no' wait to eat meat without ye lookin' as if ye will keel over," he countered. "Ye also need to rest more often. I know ye are excited to be in our new home, but ye ha' been pushin' yourself too hard."

"So your prescriptions are for me to eat more and sleep more." I snuggled against him. "I can do both of those things."

"Promise me."

"I promise." I laid against him for a moment. "I don't mean to be obstinate. I know that the baby's health comes first, but this is all new to me. It's hard to rely on someone else when I've only had myself for so long, and soon Faith will be here and she'll need us for everything, and..."

"And?" Robert prompted, when I fell silent.

"What if I'm not a good mother? I mean, I've never wanted kids. I've never been around kids or babies." I fisted my hand in his shirt. "What if I don't have any maternal instincts?"

"When ye think on Faith, what comes to mind?"

"That I'd do anything for her," I replied without hesitation. "That I would move an actual mountain if she needed me to."

"Sounds as if ye already love our wee lass."

I looked up at him. "Will that be enough?"

"Of course it will." Robert smoothed back my hair. "More than anything, bairns need love. Everything else will work itself out."

I burrowed into his arms. "I'm glad you've already had kids. At least one of us knows what we're doing."

Robert kissed my hair. "I am here for ye, for whatever ye need."

"I think our first need is to fix Doon Hill." I did not want to raise a child near the Wild Court. "What did you want me to see in the toolbox?"

"For one, 'tis a fair sight larger within that without," he replied. "I suspected it was an enchanted item from the start, but when I looked within I saw shelves stretching down as far as me eyes could see."

"I guess it really does have any tool we might need. I hope there's a legend, so we know where to find stuff."

"Aye, otherwise 'twill take a bit o' time. Speakin' o' which." Robert shifted me so my butt was on the couch instead of his leg, then he crossed the room and grabbed a notebook and pencil. "I would like ye to write down the medical specialty ye mentioned earlier."

"Okay." After I scribbled "obstetrician" on the page, I asked, "Why?"

"Ye are going to eat, and then ye are going to bed. I will find one o' these doctors in the village and make us an appointment."

"Really? Wait, how are you going to find one?" I almost added that Robert didn't know how to use Google, but he already knew that.

He shrugged. "Ask a neighbor, something like that."

"Bring me my laptop. It won't take long," I added when he gave me a look. Once I had my computer, I called up a list of obstetricians within a ten-mile radius.

"Here you go," I said, handing him the laptop. "You call, I'll sleep."

"Eat something first."

"Okay. I will make toast and then sleep. Deal?"

He kissed my hand. "Deal."

THE FUTURE

I woke up later than usual the next morning, with sunlight streaming onto my face and my body wrapped in the hotel's crisp bed sheets. The front desk hadn't minded when I'd asked to extend our stay from two nights to three. We didn't really need the third night, since our business in the area had finished once we'd set Meg and the other giants free, but the cottage in Crail was so small, and I wanted to be alone with Anya.

I rolled over and gazed at her sleeping beside me, her face so calm after all of yesterday's commotion. Maybe we could stay here forever, alone and away from the rest of the world and its problems.

Anya and I hadn't had a lot of alone time; hell, we hadn't even known each other for very long. After Rina had made the choice to leave New York—a choice she didn't need to make, but she's as stubborn as our father ever was—and I'd decided to come back to Scotland with her, Anya had all but moved into my apartment. Over the next few weeks, we'd spent almost every minute together, talking, laughing, and learning about each other.

And having sex. There had been a lot of sex.

There had been a lot of sex last night, too.

All of that aside, I couldn't remember a time in my life I'd ever fallen so hard and fast for anything. When I'd met my ex-fiancée, Olivia, I'd been attracted to her right away, but love was something that had taken months to grow between us. Even when I'd been enthralled by Nicnevin it hadn't been love, and no matter how deep I fell into her magic, I'd known it wasn't right.

Anya felt right.

If Beira tries to get between us again, I don't know what I'll do.

I moved onto my back and scrubbed my face with my hands. I understood Beira's trepidation about me, a man recently infatuated with her rival that was now sleeping with her daughter. If I was Anya's parent, I wouldn't trust me, either. But I had completed the task Beira had set for me, and her friend Meg—assuming Meg and Beira were truly friends and I hadn't just loosed a super-sized demoness back into the world—had said that she owed me. If I had to, I'd call that debt, if for no other reason than to keep Beira out of my relationship with Anya.

Anya blinked herself awake and smiled at me. My heart did a little somersault. "Good morning, beautiful."

"And a good morning to you." She pressed herself against my side. I kissed the top of her head. "What are you thinking about?"

"What makes you think I'm thinking about anything?"

"You're wearing your thoughtful face."

I wondered what my thoughtful face looked like. "If you must know, I was thinking that I'd like to get a place for just the two of us. Rina and Rob are great and all, but that cottage is awful tiny."

"Aye, it's a small but lovely home." Her fingertips traced tiny circles on my chest. "We can always spend time in my flat."

"I thought your place was in New York," I began, then I came to a less than ideal conclusion. "You don't live with your mother, do you?"

Anya burst into laughter. "I do not," she said, wiping tears from her eyes. "I keep a flat in Glasgow."

"*Glaz goh*," I repeated, imitating Anya's accent. "It's a nice flat?"

"My mother hardly ever goes there," Anya replied, thus telling me all I needed to know about the place. "It's quite far from Crail, so I imagine we can't spend all our time there. Won't you miss your sister?"

"I don't mind staying with Rob and Rina, for now," I said. "But when the baby comes, they'll need our room."

"Ah, yes. The bairn." Anya's fingers danced across my chest until she was stroking my neck. "Perhaps then we should get a flat of our own near to them? It's good to be close to family, and I would like to look in on the bairn often."

I glanced down at her. "You like babies?"

"I adore them."

"Huh." I kissed her forehead again. "There's something I hadn't thought of."

"What? The future?"

I hadn't thought about anything beyond Anya and I driving back to Crail, and me dodging my agent's next phone call. Instead of owning up to my poor planning skills, I asked, "Can I ask you a question? Or series of questions?"

"Yes, to both."

"How do you grow and shrink?"

Anya laughed softly. Her warm breath on my skin was driving me crazy. "As I told you, my father was a giant, and my mother... Well, you know all about her. Some combination of her magic and his gigantism means I can make myself large or small at will."

"Wow. So you just," I snapped my fingers, "change like that?"

"Yes, and no. It looks simple, but it took me a very, very long time to master. It also uses up a lot of energy, which is why I eat so much. That, and I like cake."

"I'd like to cover you in chocolate."

"What was that?"

"And your claws," I continued; when I'd watched Anya fight Demeter and her *drakaina* back in New York, ten wicked claws had extended from her fingers. "Is that part of being a giant, too? I didn't see claws on any of the others."

"The claws are all Beira," Anya replied. "She has an affinity with wolves. Seems she passed that bit on to me."

"Wolves." I stroked her hair. "You said your father *was* a giant. Is he gone?"

"Not hardly, but he's in no condition to talk with me." She worried the edge of the blanket. "He was turned to stone, along with all of my brothers, some time ago."

"I'm sorry," I said as I squeezed her close. Losing a parent was a feeling I was all too familiar with. "Wait, where are they? Are they in the giants' caves?"

"They're up in Scotland, near the bens they loved," Anya replied.

"Do you miss them?"

"Aye. Every day."

"After we report back to Beira, we should go visit them. Maybe we can release them, too."

Anya sat up and stared at me. "You'd help me do that?"

"Of course." I took her hands in mine. "Maybe we're meant to save them. Maybe Beira sent us here to learn how to release Meg so we could learn how to save your family."

Anya's eyes went glassy. "Oh, Christopher," she said, then she wrapped her arms around me, and that was the last we said about giants for a long while.

CLOSURE

"There's the bairn," Dr. Khanna said. "Can you see 'em?"

"I see her." I was lying on a paper-covered examination table with my shirt shoved up past my ribs, and cold jelly spread across my abdomen. Robert had outdone himself, since while I'd napped and nibbled on snacks the day prior he'd gotten us an appointment with an obstetrician first thing in the morning. No one gets things done like a gallowglass.

The medical center was walking distance from our cottage, and they were affiliated with the local hospital, which was excellent since Faith would probably be born there. The staff at the medical center was super nice, and after they'd asked us all of the routine questions and done some bloodwork, Dr. Khanna asked if I'd had a recent ultrasound. I hadn't, so the doctor ushered us right into the ultrasound room and set to work.

Now, Robert and I were staring with rapt attention at a black and white monitor, watching Faith as she hung out in my belly.

"She's so big." I could see her head, her torso, and her arms and legs; she was a person. A real, actual person. Even with all the research I'd done, I hadn't expected her to look so developed, or for a fuzzy gray image to make my heart feel overfull.

"She's perfect," Robert said. "She is, isn't she? Do ye detect anythin' out o' the ordinary?"

"This baby looks perfect to me." Dr. Khanna moved the ultrasound wand to give us a slightly different view. "I see no cause for concern, just a very healthy fetus. Based on the measurements, you're about fifteen weeks along."

"Fifteen weeks?" I repeated. "Then I'm in my second trimester. I hadn't thought I was that far. Everything's happening so fast."

Robert squeezed my hand. For a man whose last child was born in the seventeenth century, he was doing pretty well with the modern medical equipment. "We've more than half left to go."

"He's right about that," Dr. Khanna said. "Would you like to know the gender?"

"It's a girl," I said.

Dr. Khanna smiled. "Good guess."

The rest of the appointment was a blur, and soon enough Robert and I were walking home, each of us clutching little printouts of Faith's ultrasound image.

"That was magical," I said. "I know we're around magic all the time, but seeing Faith was amazing."

"One o' the best moments o' me life." Robert shifted the bag he was carrying to his other hand. We'd purchased two orders of fish and chips for lunch, since the chipper was on the way home from the clinic, and the baby didn't object to fish the way she did to beef or chicken. "As much as I regret mentionin' it, we do have something else to attend to."

I sighed. "All right. After we eat, we'll deal with Doon Hill."

Our lunch wasn't one of the better meals we'd had, but it did the job. After we ate, and I'd taken my Robert-mandated one hour nap, we both sat in the middle of the great room's floor on either side of Dougal's tool box. I peeked inside the box, and it was just as Robert had described: shelves and shelves of tools extending downward as far as the eye could see.

"Whoa," I said, leaning back. "That view's making me dizzy."

"What's more is that I can no' locate the same item twice," Robert said. "The same sort o' tool, yes, but if I return a tool to the box it's ne'er to be seen again."

I suppose that explained why there was a pile of implements underneath the coffee table ranging from files to hand-cranked drills. Robert had set aside anything he'd thought might be useful. "Is there a common theme, at least?"

"The items the box decides to reveal to us are haphazard at best."

"Huh." I grabbed a marble from the latest tray of surprises the box had offered up and dropped it inside. I counted to thirty and then gave up, but I never did hear the marble hit bottom.

"Is this thing a pocket dimension?" I lifted the edge and looked at the underside; it was smooth, solid metal coated in red enamel paint. "It doesn't even weigh that much."

"'Tis a mystery, that's certain."

I set the box back down and tapped the side. Solid as a rock. "Have you asked it to give you the right tool?"

"I am no' in the habit o' askin' inanimate objects for anything."

"Now seems like a great time to start." I traced the edge of the open box with my fingertip. "The first time I opened a portal, I spoke to a tree. Basically, I asked it to let you out. Maybe we just need to tell the box what we need."

"All right. Give it a go."

"Me? Why me?"

"You are the only walker present."

I took a deep breath, and said, "Hello. Tool box? Hi, I'm Rina. This is Robert." Robert shook his head, but I pressed onward. "We've got a door that won't stay shut. Do you have anything that can help us fix it?" The box sat there. As boxes do. "Please?"

The box shuddered a bit, then there was a metallic sound like gears turning from far below. A tray like all the trays that had come before rose up from the depths. This tray was empty, save for a wooden door wedge perched in the center.

Robert laughed out loud. "O' course, a simple solution is usually best. Karina me love, we shall wedge the door on Doon Hill shut, and then it shall trouble us no more."

I picked up the wedge and turned it over; it was just a simple hunk of wood, our simple solution to a complex problem. Brilliant. "All right. Let's do it."

Our second drive from Crail to Aberfoyle was rather uneventful. In fact, it was so boring I was glad Robert had ordered me to take a nap earlier, otherwise I might have fallen asleep during the trip.

"You know, if you were driving I could be resting," I said when we were about halfway there. "Starting tomorrow, I'm giving you driving lessons."

Robert glanced at the steering wheel. "The village is small. We can walk everywhere we need to go."

"What about when I get too big to drive? What if you have to take me to the hospital?"

Robert made a face. "We have Christopher for such emergencies. He called while ye were sleeping. He and Anya shall return on the morrow."

"I wonder how Beira feels about that." My gaze slid toward Robert. "When Faith's old enough to date, I don't want you acting like Anya's mother."

He snorted. "I promise I will no' behave in a manner akin to the Queen o' Winter."

"I mean like an overbearing crazy man."

He reached over and took my hand. "I promise I shall do my best by her, and all our other children."

I almost went off the road. "What other children?"

Robert laughed out loud. I ignored him and concentrated on driving.

We reached the center of Aberfoyle about half an hour later. After I parked Dougal's truck, we climbed the trail to Doon Hill. The door wedge was safely tucked in the front pocket of my hooded sweatshirt, though I was still a bit concerned about our grand plan. Could a simple piece of wood really close the portal to Elphame I'd left open in the Minster's Pine?

"What do you think it'll be like up there?" I asked as the trail inclined upward.

"I reckon that the court, if ye can rightly call it that, will be a fair sight bigger than when last we encountered it," he replied. "Other than that, I can no' say."

I stopped walking. "Who is running this court?"

Robert's eyes widened. "That is a verra good question," he said. "While I would like to ken the answer, I believe it's best we close the door right away. We can continue to learn about the court and who's responsible for it afterward."

"Good plan."

We resumed walking up the trail, which was less muddy than the last time we'd trekked up the hill. As pieces of good fortune went, it was a small one, but it was better than nothing.

I heard the commotion of the court's followers long before I saw them. Robert motioned for me to wait, then he crept toward the clearing to ascertain the situation. When he returned to my side, he was frowning.

"There must be a thousand o' those beasties, all packed 'round the Pine like bees swarmin' a hive," he said. "If there were maybe half as many we could take advantage of the fact that mortal aren't supposed to see the Good People and walk straight by them, but with those numbers there is no way we could avoid bumpin' into a few o' them."

"Even if we could get across the clearing, I can't shut the door with all of them packed around the tree. What we need is a distraction." I looked at Robert, and realized something: gallowglasses are damn distracting. "Pretty much all of the fairies know who you are, right? And that you're the Seelie King's champion?"

A smile spread across his face as he understood where my plan was going. "Aye, that they do." He extended his arm to the side, and a moment later, his claymore appeared in his hand and his shield was strapped to his back. His armor, chain mail over a heavy leather tunic and pants, replaced his modern clothing, but I noticed he kept his new hiking boots.

"Why the boots?" I asked.

"Better traction, and far more comfortable. Doctors aren't the only professionals who've made advancements since my day." Robert pulled me close and tilted up my chin. "I will draw them away from the Pine, then you shall enter the clearing and close the door. We shall meet at the truck."

"Okay. Be careful."

He kissed me softly, sweetly. "Don't do anything foolish."

"It's a little late for that."

Robert grinned, then he put on his helm and circled around through the trees to the far side of the clearing. The hill top must have grown in size since our last visit, because almost five full minutes went by before I heard him yelling and beating his sword against his shield.

"Hear me," Robert bellowed. "I am the gallowglass, and I am here to return ye whence ye came!"

The fae scattered, melting into the trees and pelting down the trail. I pressed myself against a tree alongside the entrance to the clearing, holding myself still as a statue as they swarmed around and over me, dragging their wings and hair and God knew what else across my body.

Once the trail was clear of fleeing fairies, I headed toward the hill crest and the Minister's Pine. When I stepped onto the relatively flat clearing I saw that while it wasn't empty, the few fairies that were still present didn't seem concerned with what one lone human was up to. I took advantage of that, and made a beeline toward the pine.

"Karina, what are ye doing here?" Uncle John asked as he stepped in front of me.

"Sightseeing." I heard the clang of metal. "Robert's just over there if you'd like to say hello."

"Staying out of the gallowglass's way has always been in me best interests," he replied. "Who sent ye here?"

"No one. I drove myself."

John didn't buy that for a second. "Was it the Seelie King? Why has the gallowglass been sent to round us up? We're not doing anything wrong here."

"Really? So sneaking out of Nicnevin's court and building a new one behind her back isn't the least bit shady?" I crossed my arms over my chest. "Why don't you tell me exactly what's going on here? Maybe I'll plead your case to Fionnlagh."

"We're tryin' to bring magic back to the world." He leaned closer, and added, "Don't ye want to be a part o' that? Ye could be a queen."

I stepped back from him. "Magic is gone for a reason. Fae don't do well with all the iron used in modern infrastructures. If you bring too many into the world, they'll die, and what good will that do?"

"They will no' die if they consume me elixir." From his coat pocket, he withdrew a clear glass bottle with a cork stopper. It was filled with a bright green, slightly frothy liquid that looked so much like what people thought an alchemist's potion should be, it could have been a movie prop. "Ye know the arts as well. We can both sell the elixir, start up a family business if ye like."

"I do not like." I walked around him and put my hand on the pine. "Is this your latest get rich quick scheme, to trick the Good People into being indebted to you? That's terrible!"

"Can't ye see what this could mean for me?" John cried.

"I get it. I really do." I took the final step toward the Minister's Pine, and laid my hand on the trunk. "Hang on, I need to do something."

I closed my eyes, shutting out John and the remaining fae and concentrated on how the Pine felt underneath my hand. It was rough, but not uncomfortable, the bark having been smoothed over by untold raindrops and windy days. I remembered how I'd felt the first time I'd touched the Minister's Pine, before I'd known about Seelie Courts and gallowglasses. I'd been lost then, feeling unsure about the choices I'd made and my future. But the Pine... The Pine had been solid. Certain. Laying my hand on the bark had centered me then, and it did so again.

"Show me the door," I said, and in my mind's eye I saw the door to Elphame cut deep within the living wood. It mirrored the shape of the trunk, with the bottom edge aligned with a hollow near the tree's roots. The doorway had started with a crack, but I could see how others had worked away at it, worrying at the opening until it could admit bigger and bigger creatures. Worst of all, all of this traveling between worlds had taken its toll on the tree. It was hurting.

"I'm so sorry," I said to the tree. "I never meant for any of this to happen. Can you help me close the way, once and for all?"

"Karina, do no' do this," John yelled. I ignored him as I knelt down and shoved the wedge into the hollow.

The tree shuddered, and the light dissipated. When I reached out again, I confirmed it: the door was closed, and in time the tree would heal.

"Thank you." I patted the trunk and got to my feet. John grabbed my shoulder and spun me around. My back hit the trunk and I stumbled.

"Why didn't ye heed me?" he demanded. His face was beet red and spittle was flying everywhere. "Do ye ken how rare such portals are? It took me decades to find this one!"

"Maybe they're rare for a reason," I said. I glanced around the clearing, but none of the few creatures that remained were interested in what John and I were arguing about. I guessed that was good.

I also didn't hear any sounds of fighting, which was not so good. Robert had said that we would meet at the truck, and if he'd already scared off the bulk of the fae, he was probably halfway to the car park. Granted, I was certain he'd double back when he got to the truck and saw that I wasn't there, but who knew how long that would take.

Meanwhile, my crazy pseudo-uncle was staring at me with murder in his eyes. "If ye won't reopen this door, ye can always create me a new one," he said. "Me mistress will be ever so pleased."

Mistress? "So you are working for Nicnevin!"

John laughed. "Close, but no. Be a good girl now, make me a new door and I will present ye to me mistress straight aways."

"That's not how being a walker works."

"Isn't it? 'Tis how it has worked for every other walker I've known. Most were quite willing to help, or at least accept payment for their work."

"I-I can't do that."

"Do ye not ken the way?" When I stayed silent, he asked, "What, do ye no' understand the reach o' your own power? I can teach ye."

"Can you?"

"O' course. What is family for if no' to help each other in our time o' need?"

John smiled at me, and I didn't know if I should be impressed with my amateur acting ability or pissed that he thought I was that dumb. He stepped back and gestured toward the clearing, saying something about how we'd put the new, larger door in a better location, and how we'd be treated like royalty wherever we went. As soon as I had a clear line to the trail down the hill, I ran.

"Karina," John screamed after me, but I kept going. I made it to the trail and slid on a wet patch, but I kept myself upright. I scrambled to regain my footing and ran again, jumping over roots and all the offerings that littered the trail, my head down as I navigated the terrain. I kept running until I ran straight into Robert.

"I have ye," Robert said. He set his hands on my shoulders, his forehead creased as he looked over my sweating, panting self. "You're runnin' as if the devil himself is at your back."

"Not the devil," I said as I panted. "John. He wanted to me to make a new door. This," I gestured toward the hill, "is all him and the woman he's working for."

"Nicnevin?"

I shook my head. "That's what I thought, but John claims he's working for someone else."

I felt Robert's back straighten. "Get behind me, love," he said. I followed his gaze up the trail and saw John standing there.

"Go no further," Robert said. "Your business with Karina is done."

"Ye can no' order me away from me own niece," John said. "We're family! What are ye to her, anyway? Just a souvenir from Elphame, nothin' more. Plenty more where the likes o' ye came from."

"All ye need to ken is this," Robert began. "I defend Karina with me sword and me body. I am lettin' ye live today because ye are her relation, but rest assured that if ye contact her again, I will have your head."

Robert turned on his heel, then he scooped me up and walked down the trail and away from John.

"Is he still there?" Robert asked.

I peeked over his shoulder. "Nope. No one's behind us."

"Good."

"I can walk, you know," I said.

"After all the runnin' ye did ye need to rest," Robert said.

"I'm fine."

"Ye certainly are, and I am goin' to keep ye that way."

I sighed and laid my head against his shoulder. There were worse fates than being carried across the countryside by a handsome man. I closed my eyes and let the cadence of Robert's footsteps lull me to sleep.

LACY'S CAVES

Anya and I slept in the next morning. Room service had delivered a tray of coffee and pastries to us early on, which we drank and devoured in bed. After our breakfast, we pressed against each other, both of us drowsy and warm. It wasn't long before Anya was sleeping in my arms. I wanted to sleep too, but I couldn't. Something was wrong about Long Meg, and I couldn't figure out what it was.

It wasn't just the inherent weirdness of a woman—not an ordinary woman, but a *giantess*—being trapped inside a stone, or even all the other giants we'd freed from the churchyard. Nor was it just that Beira had thought my uncle, John Damian, had imprisoned Meg, when it was apparently a widely accepted fact that the long-deceased Michael Scot was the man responsible. This whole situation was off, and I needed to figure out what Beira's plan really was.

I slid out of bed and turned on my laptop. Usually I would have checked my email right away, but I'd decided to continue avoiding Maisie and all book-related items, at least until I was back in Crail. Instead, I started researching Long Meg, Michael Scot, and anything else I thought might be connected to my present circumstances. After an hour of fruitless investigation, I searched for the giants' caves I'd read about in the tourist brochures at the hotel's front desk. The third article I read gave me a lead.

"Anya." I gently shook her shoulder. Her eyes fluttered open, and she smiled at me. "Want to go for a walk?"

"I thought we were staying in bed today."

"Bed's not going anywhere. It'll be here when we get back."

She sat up and stretched, letting the sheets puddle around her waist as she gazed at me with mournful gray eyes. "But the pillows are so soft."

"They are. And so are the blankets, and the mattress, and I know I'll miss them terribly." I stood and extended my hand. She accepted it, and I pulled her upright. "While you were sleeping, I did a bit of research about the area. There are some caves I want to check out."

"Oh, you mean the Giants' Cave?"

"Nope. I found us a whole new set of caves to investigate."

Anya shook her head. "Your sister is rubbing off on you, both in research habits and speech. This will be quite an adventure."

Two hours later found Anya and me trekking across the countryside, very close to the field where we'd spent the past few days. During my research, I'd learned that Long Meg and Her Daughters were a stop on a popular circular walking trail. Other sites on the walk included an abandoned mine, a rail line, and a spot called Lacy's Caves. The caves were named after an eighteenth century man who'd ordered them dug, and who had then tried to blow up Long Meg.

You read that right.

"I think I see them up ahead," I said. We were walking along a narrow trail that ran alongside the River Eden. The caves themselves were perched right on the edge of the riverbank and a steep drop; one wrong step and you'd be getting wet. I'd read that the man responsible for them, a Lieutenant Colonel Samuel Lacy, once used this spot for entertaining. I wondered how many of his guests had ended up taking a dip.

The caves themselves were quite a sight. They were carved from red sandstone, and they had gently curved rooflines reminiscent of what cartoon woodland creatures might call home. We stepped inside the caves, and found five chambers that extended back into the hillside. The entrances were grand pointed arches, giving the site a cathedral-like effect.

Other than the cave's natural ambiance, they were empty. There wasn't even any trash left behind by inconsiderate tourists. While that was nice, it wasn't helping me.

"What were you hoping to learn in these caverns?" Anya asked; during the walk I'd told her that something didn't feel right about how we'd freed Meg, and Anya agreed that the whole situation was off. "There's precious little of anything here."

"They say Colonel Lacy tried blowing up Meg and the rest of the circle so he could plow the field, but that doesn't make sense," I replied. "The circle is huge. Couldn't he have just planted crops around the stones, or just used the field for grazing, like it's used now? He must have wanted the stones destroyed for a different reason."

Anya trailed her fingertips along a darker vein of sandstone in the cave wall. "Those remembered by history rarely do things that make sense. Perhaps he had a surplus of gunpowder and got bored one day."

I shook my head. "When they were setting up the explosives, a thunderstorm came out of nowhere and the workers went running for cover. That storm changed Lacy's entire attitude about Meg. He went from wanting the stones gone to wanting to immortalize them. He even commissioned paintings of the site."

Anya's brow arched. "You think something otherworldly drove him off?"

"I do." I stood in one of the front arches overlooking the river. The surrounding area was called Eden Valley, and it lived up to its name. "Did Beira have anything to do with that storm?"

"How would I know?"

"Don't you remember it?" When she remained silent, I turned around. She was standing in the middle of the chamber, arms crossed over her breast and frowning.

"How old do you think I am?" she demanded.

"I have no idea," I replied. "Aren't you immortal? I thought..." I let my head droop and rubbed my eyes. "That was insensitive, wasn't it?"

"A bit."

"I'm sorry. This is still new to me, you know? Not that this being new is an excuse," I added. "I thought immortality came with the whole fairy package."

Anya's eyebrows arched higher on her forehead. "You don't know what I am, do you?"

I started to protest, then I realized she was right. "No, I don't."

She worried her lower lip for a moment, then she leaned against the cave wall. "As you know, my father is a giant. And no, giants are not fairies."

"What's the difference? Other than size," I asked.

"The difference is in where they—we—originate. Fairies are beings that slipped through from Elphame, whereas giants are creatures born of this realm."

"Huh. So that means giants are kind of like big, tall humans?"

A smile spread across her face. "Exactly."

"What about Beira? I always assumed she was like Nicnevin." Anya made a face. Comparing her mother to the Seelie Queen wasn't the best analogy I'd ever come up with. "I mean, since your mother is a magical queen, and Nicnevin is the Seelie Queen."

"I understand your meaning, and yes, I do understand why you find them similar, on the surface, at least. Mum is also of this realm and is the personification of winter, whereas the Seelie are the residents of Elphame."

I noticed that she said "Seelie", not "Nicnevin" or "the Seelie Queen." "Is Nicnevin not a fairy, either?"

"Nicnevin is something else entirely." She ducked her head. "As am I."

I cupped her face with my hands. "I like what you are."

She brushed her lips against mine. "I like what you are, too."

"So you're not a thousand year old fairy?"

She laughed against my lips. "Not hardly. I was born shortly before magic left this world, during what your kind calls the Industrial Revolution. We're long lived, but not immortal." She leaned back and regarded me. "Now you need to tell me how many years you've seen. It's only fair."

"Me? I'm thirty-three." I stroked my thumbs across her cheekbones. "I've never dated an older woman before."

"Dating?" Laughter bubble up from her throat. "Is that what we're doing?"

I gestured at the cavern's arched ceiling. "I do take you to all the best places."

We laughed together, and then we kissed for a little while. Caves were conducive to romance, who knew? After a time, we ended up sitting in one of the archways, watching the River Eden rush by.

"Christopher," Anya began, "do you really think there's something more to us freeing Meg?"

"There must be, but I have no idea what it could be," I replied. "Maybe your mother just missed her friend, and I'm reading into things."

She wrapped her arms around one of mine and laid her head on my shoulder. "Or perhaps you've seen the edge of a larger plan. Mum doesn't share everything with me; och, she still sees me as a wee lass, not a woman grown."

I kissed her hair. "I see you as a woman."

"I know you do." She tightened her grip on my arm. "Just as I know that whatever forces are at work will reveal themselves in time. We only need to be patient."

"Easy for you to say. You're three hundred years old."

"Keep it up, and you may not see thirty-four."

FOUL SMELLING BEAN PASTE

The next time I opened my eyes, I was lying on the lumpy old couch in the cottage. My favorite pillow was under my head, and the comforter from our bed was tucked around me. I was so warm and comfortable, I never wanted to move again.

Then I realized that I had absolutely no recollection of driving home.

"Robert?"

"Over here."

I sat up, and saw him milling about in the kitchen. He stopped what he was doing when I said his name, poured a cup of coffee and brought it over to me.

"Thank you." I sipped the hot beverage while Robert sat in front of me on the coffee table. "How long have I been out?"

"About three hours now. Ye slept the whole ride back from Aberfoyle."

I froze with the mug halfway to my mouth. "If I was sleeping, how did we get home?"

"I drove the truck," he replied, as if that wasn't completely impossible.

"What?" I set down the mug and stared at him. Since that first day on Doon Hill, I'd been operating under the assumption that Robert was one of the most intelligent people I'd ever met. Well, you know what happens when you assume. "But you don't have a license. And you don't know how to drive!"

He shrugged. The man who had illegally driven across half of Scotland shrugged. "I have watched ye drive often enough. 'Twas no' that difficult."

"If you had been stopped you would have gone to jail!"

He grinned. "But I was no' stopped, and if I were, I would have appealed to the officer's sense o' decency. Ye are lovely when ye sleep, Karina lass, and he would have agreed that only a heartless man would have woken ye."

"Where I come from, not all cops have a sense of decency. Most are good, but some are total jerks."

"Then 'tis just as well we returned to our island," he replied. This nonchalant attitude was driving me nuts. "All is well, Karina me love."

I glared at him, which just made his grin widen. "Anyway. I'm glad you made some coffee, but I'm starved. Want to order something?"

"No' from that chipper we patronized earlier."

I made a face. "That was pretty awful." I gazed longingly at the empty kitchen cabinets. "Eventually, we are going to have to go shopping."

"Or perhaps we already have all we need." Robert retrieved the cornucopia from the shelf above the fireplace and set it on the coffee table. I made room for him on the couch and he sat beside me. "The purpose o' this basket is to provide pleasures and abundance, such as good food. Perhaps it works much like the toolbox, and we need only make a request."

"Makes as much sense as anything else does around here." Which wasn't much. "Have you tried it yet?"

Robert shook his head. "I wanted to wait for ye."

He really was the sweetest man. "What do you want to ask it for?"

"What I would really like is a joint o' mutton, roasted o'er the fire until the edges are charred just a wee bit."

I shuddered. "All right. Mutton it up." Robert got up and walked toward the kitchen cabinets. "What are you doing?"

"I thought we'd best have plates on hand. No tellin' how this food will arrive." He set the plates on the coffee table and regarded the cornucopia. "I'd like some mutton please," he said, then he reached inside the tiny woven basket and withdrew a juicy portion of roast mutton.

"Will you look at that." I leaned forward and examined the meat, my fascination temporarily overriding my disgust at the meat stink wafting toward me. "Try it."

I didn't have to tell him twice. Robert took a huge bite of mutton, and grinned while he chewed. "Perfect," he said after he swallowed. "Now ye."

"Okay. Um. May I have some carrot sticks and hummus?"

"Hummus?" Robert repeated. "Ye can have any food imaginable, and ye ask for that foul smellin' bean paste?"

"I like hummus." I reached into the cornucopia, and felt something hard and round. I withdrew a white ceramic bowl filled with hummus. When I reached inside it again, I found a second bowl. That one was full of carrot sticks.

"This is awesome," I said as I swirled a carrot stick in the hummus. "Do you think the food on demand feature lasts indefinitely, or do we only get so many requests?"

"I suppose we shall find out, one way or the other."

Robert ate his mutton while I crunched away on my carrot sticks. Once I'd taken the edge off my hunger, I got up and put my leftovers in the fridge.

"I'm going to take a shower," I announced. I went into our bedroom and kicked off my shoes and socks while I observed the overflowing hamper. While we'd gotten a temporary reprieve on grocery shopping, someone was going to have to do the laundry.

I pulled my hoodie up and over my head and tossed it on top of the dresser. When I opened my eyes and looked at the mirror, I saw Robert standing behind me.

"Hey."

"Hey, yourself." Robert tugged on my hairband and loosened my ponytail. He ran his fingers through my hair, straightening the long brown strands against my shoulders.

"Did you follow me in here just to play with my hair?" I leaned back against him, and enjoyed his attentions.

A lazy grin, blue eyes at half-mast. "No' just your hair."

Watching our reflections, Robert abandoned my hair as he slid his hands around my waist and framed my belly. I'd only been wearing a thin cotton shirt under my hoodie, and his warm hands were like a brand on my skin. "Still so small," Robert murmured. "When we saw her on that machine, it felt like she'd be here in a trice."

"I know." I reached back and tangled my fingers in the dark, soft hair right above the nape of his neck. He hadn't cut it since right after New Year's, and I liked twisting my fingers in it. "Think she'll be tall like you?"

"I wonder if she'll be a scholar," Robert mused. "Imagine if we had a child who hated books."

"Not everyone is cut out for higher learning. Maybe she'll race cars instead."

"Driving is fun," he said with a devilish grin that had no place on a reverend.

"You need a license before you try that again!"

"All right. I'll get one." He slid his hands underneath my shirt and cupped my breasts. I stood on my toes and arched my neck. Robert took the invitation and kissed the sensitive spot where my neck met my shoulder.

"Karina." His warm breath made me shiver. I twisted around in his arms and kissed him hard. He upped the ante by picking me up, his hands firm beneath my thighs, and bringing me to bed.

Afterward, we lounged in bed, spooning like some old married couple. Robert's big hand was on my belly as he desperately searched for Faith's kicks.

"I think it's still too early for that." I placed my hand over his. "She'll kick soon."

"Soon." Robert kissed the back of my neck. "Karina, I..."

He didn't finish his thought. After a few seconds, I rolled over and faced him. "What's wrong?"

"No' a thing. It's just..." He gathered me against him, tucking my face against his neck. "Ye scare me so much, love. When ye were runnin' down the trail, I feared the worst."

"I was okay." I drew back and found his eyes with mine. "I'm sorry I scared you. I didn't mean to."

"I ken that. I also ken that perhaps I need to make peace wi' bein' a little scared from time to time." He smoothed back my hair and kissed my forehead. "I've said it before, ye are the strongest person I have ever met. What ye see in me, I will ne'er understand."

"You know what I see in you. You're the gallowglass, feared throughout this world and Elphame. As long as I keep you around, no one will mess with me."

"So ye like me for me sword?"

"Yes." My hand strayed lower. "Your sword is excellent."

"Karina!"

"What? Like you're embarrassed." I nudged him onto his back and folded my arms on top of his chest. "Do you even get embarrassed anymore?"

Robert laughed his deep, melodious laugh. Until that moment I hadn't realized he hadn't laughed that way since before he was summoned to act as Fionnlagh's champion and he ended up facing the Hydra. "I believe I lost all capacity for shame some time ago."

"Can I ask you something?"

"Yes. Anything."

"When Fionnlagh sent you to fight the Hydra, what else happened?" His gaze left mine, and I almost regretted my question. We'd never talked about what he'd gone through before I found him and brought him back to this dimension.

"Bad things, then terrible things," he said at last.

"Was it worse that being Nicnevin's prisoner?"

"No. When I was Nicnevin's servant, I was a desperate man living on the last shreds o' hope. This past time, I had you. I kent that e'en if I could no' defeat the monsters set against me, ye were out there lookin' for a way to free me. I kent ye would rescue me if I could no' rescue myself."

"I will always find you," I said.

"And I, you."

I laid my head on his chest and laced my fingers with his. "Partners. We're in this together."

"Aye, love. Partners."

POWERFUL FORCES

The next morning, Robert and I were still tangled together in the bedsheets, a warm heap of arms and legs and happiness. Even though we slept together every night, last night had been different. I felt like I had truly been with Robert—the real Robert, not the mask he wore around others—for the first time in weeks. Maybe that was the first time he'd ever let me really see him. I was honored he trusted me that much.

After we'd kissed and cuddled for a bit, Robert asked me how I'd like to spend the day. "I'm afraid I know what we need to do," I said, nodding toward our laundry. "It's either wash the clothes we own or buy new ones."

"Perhaps Dougal's toolbox has a washer woman in its depths?"

"If only." I reached for my phone on the bedside table.

"Who are ye callin'?"

"I'm searching for a plumber," I replied. "Maybe we can get a washing machine installed here. It would make things way easier, especially when the baby comes."

"Baby." Robert grinned, then he slid down my body and kissed my small but present bump. "*Mo leanabh. Chan urrainn dhomh feitheamh gus coinneachadh riut.*"

I tossed my phone toward the far side of the bed. "What did you say?"

"I told her I can't wait to meet her."

I caressed Robert's cheek. He turned his head and kissed my palm. "I like it when you speak Gaelic. Makes me all warm and fuzzy."

"Does it, now." He slid his hands underneath my hips, then he kissed the inside of my thigh. "*Tha gaol agam ort.*"

"I love you, too."

Later still, I stepped out of the steam-filled bathroom, wrapped in my robe while I towel dried my hair. The shower had been bone-meltingly hot, and the warmth and steam had worked out all of my lingering muscle aches from walking up and then running back down Doon Hill.

The water had been too hot for Robert, who muttered something about having already been to plenty of hell dimensions before he abandoned me in the bathroom. I found him in the living room, already dressed and pulling on his boots.

"Are we going somewhere?" I asked.

"I thought I'd go down to the market and pick up a few things," he replied. "After all, we do no' want to take advantage o' Persephone's gift."

"Want me to go with you?"

"If ye like. Or," he added as he pulled me into his arms, "ye can stay here, warm and cozy, and await my return."

"Okay." I kissed him. "Get eggs. And orange juice."

"Aye, love. Be back in two shakes of a lamb's tail."

Robert left for the market, and I got myself dressed. Since I could no longer button any of my jeans, not even the baggy pair, I put on a pair of black leggings. To that I added an old knit shirt, wool socks, and my favorite hoodie from the day before. I didn't look very fashionable, but I was definitely cozy.

Once that was done, I began the odious task separating our laundry. I got through half of it before I decided that hiring a plumber would be a better use of my time. I wandered out of the bedroom and into the living area, wondering where we'd put a washer. Maybe we'd have to build an addition? We could do that, since we had plenty of land to work with. The cottage sat on just over three acres. In the midst of my musings I walked by the cornucopia, which was still sitting on the coffee table where we'd left it the night before. My stomach growled as soon as I set eyes on it.

"One more request won't hurt," I said as I sat in front of it. "Cornucopia? Could I please have a cannoli?"

The charmed object promptly delivered a cannoli as perfect as any I'd ever eaten in Queens. I wondered if Persephone had used baked goods to gain followers back in the day. If so, sign me up.

"I miss Persephone," I said to the cornucopia, because talking to magical baskets was a totally normal thing to do. I picked it up and turned it over, examining the tightly woven reeds. "Maybe I can invite her and Andreas to come visit. That would be fun, like a little reunion. I wonder if they'll bring Hades? I bet he can do some great party tricks."

Someone knocked on the front door. I figured that Robert had locked the door when he left for the market and then forgotten his key, or maybe Chris and Anya were back with stories about Englishmen and giants, fee fie fo fum and all. I stashed the cornucopia in my hoodie's front pocket and went to open the door. Standing on my front stoop was John Damian.

"You're here, because?" I braced the door with my foot, and kept it from opening wider than a few inches.

"I have come to offer my sincerest apologies," John said. "I was in quite a state on the hill yesterday, and not at me best."

I leaned against the door frame. "Go on."

"When ye closed the portal it was quite a shock, no' only to me, but many others as well. Powerful forces are invested in creating this new court."

"Oh? Exactly what forces?"

He leaned closer, as if he was sharing a great secret. "No' the Seelie, that's for sure."

"Oh, there's a great idea," I said, assuming he meant he was in with the Unseelie Court. "Let's have the evil fairies run amok among the humans." I crossed my arms over my chest and shook my head. "That's beyond irresponsible, and you know it."

John shook his head. "Ye can no' consider the Good People like ye do humans, separating them to extremes. Just like ye can no ha' summer's heat without winter's chill, ye need the light and the dark. Balance is key, ye ken."

Winter's chill. "Who's running this new, not-Unseelie Court?"

John reached inside his coat pocket. "Someone ye are already quite familiar with."

"What have you got there? An invitation or something?"

"Or something."

John withdrew his hand and flung a powder into my face. I tried shutting the door, but the powder stuck to my skin, then it was in my mouth and my nose and I couldn't breathe. It got in my eyes and they welled up with tears. I heard the wights' wings beating around my head as I slumped to the floor, then nothing.

GONE

I spent the entire drive north from Cumbria not thinking about how Beira would react when Anya and I told her we had freed Meg and the other giants. Truth be told, I wanted her to appreciate what we'd done. I also wanted her to give me a chance at proving that I was more than one of Nicnevin's castoffs, and that I would treat Anya well. The nagging voice in the back of my head told me that I had bigger questions to ask her.

Anya must have had similar thoughts. When we crossed the town line and entered Crail proper, she touched my arm. "She'll be at the pub," she said.

"Should we wait and talk to her later on?" I asked. "I don't want to bother her at work."

"The pub is better."

"All right." I turned toward the center of the village. "The pub it is."

Soon enough, we were walking into the pub; it was one of those places that was always dark inside, even when the sun was blazing away at midday. Beira noted our entry and jerked her chin toward two stools at the far end of the bar. We sat, and Beira delivered us two glasses of whisky a moment later.

"Let's hear it," Beira said.

"Christopher did as you asked," Anya began. "He freed Meg, and the rest of the giants in Penrith."

"All of them?" Beira's head tilted to the side, as if she was seeing me for the first time. "I wondered if you had it in you."

"Looks like I did," I said. I fingered my glass, but I didn't drink. "What made you think my uncle imprisoned the giants? Meg said that Michael Scot—the real one—imprisoned her, and he died a long time ago. My uncle is still alive."

"Did she say that? Names change over the years, and it's hard to keep up," Beria replied. "Plans change, too, as mine just have. Thanks to you, my guard is now complete."

"Guard?" I asked. "The giants guard things for you?"

Beira's mouth stretched, revealing teeth that sparkled like rows of diamonds. A beat too late, I realized she was smiling. "They haven't guarded anything as of yet. Go on then, the both of ye drink up. I am going to find Meg and tell her all about everything she's missed out on over the years."

Beira disappeared through the swinging doors at the far end of the bar. I glanced at Anya; her face was pinched in a frown.

"That was odd," Anya said. "She was so fired up over you, and now..." She shook her head. "Christopher, I never thought I'd say this, but I wonder if we did the right thing."

I set down the glass, leaving the whisky untouched. Something told me that consuming anything poured by Beira's hand was not in my best interests. "Let's go talk to the only person in Scotland who always has her head on straight."

"Who's that?"

"Rina."

When Anya and I pulled up to the cottage, the first thing I noticed was my BMW parked out front and waiting for me to take her out. The next item on my to-do list was completing the necessary paperwork and paying whatever customs were required, then Anya and I would take the car and explore Scotland in style. Our first stop could be her place down in Glasgow, then maybe we'd go house hunting and find a cottage of our own.

Parked next to my car was Dougal's massive black truck, which hopefully meant that Robert hadn't killed him yet. With gallow-glasses, one could never be sure. Farther down the lane, the wights were assembled in a floating mass in front of the cottage's door in a quivering, rainbow-hued herd. "What's gotten them all worked up?" I wondered.

"Who's that?" Anya asked. I looked in the rearview mirror and saw a small blue car turn down our driveway and park behind me. At first I thought whomever was in the car was lost, then Maisie fucking Perkins got out of the car and waved.

"Shit," I said.

"What's wrong?" Anya asked.

"My agent has flown in from New York to harass me in person." Even as I said the words, I could hardly believe she'd done such a thing. What kind of a lunatic hops a transatlantic flight instead of making a phone call or sending an email?

"Perhaps you should have accepted her calls," Anya said.

Someday, I'm going to ask Anya if she reads minds. "I can't imagine what she's doing here." Anya and I got out of the rental car and I jerked my chin toward the wights. "Can you find out what's up with them while I deal with her?"

"Surely."

Anya headed toward the wights as I hailed my agent. "Hi, Maisie."

"Hello, Chris," she said. Maisie was close to my age, but she had an air of disapproving elementary school teacher about her that had always made her seem much older. She was tall, with a long alpine nose at the perfect angle for her to look down upon the world, and she always wore thick-rimmed round glasses that disappeared into her mass of curly hair. "I'm glad to see you're still alive. I was beginning to wonder if you'd had an accident."

"There was the flight here and all the settling in, and then Anya and I went to England for a few days." I gestured toward Anya where she stood with the wights, and saw Maisie's brows peak. I imagined that to a regular, non-fairy seeing person it looked like Anya was waving her arms and talking to herself, instead of speaking with Wyatt and the rest of the wights.

"Would you like to come inside?" I grabbed Maisie's elbow and marched her toward the door. "Remember my sister, Rina? I'm sure she'd love to see you."

"I doubt that." Maisie craned her neck to stare at Anya as we walked by her. "When I called her the other day, she practically hung up on me."

"You called Rina?" I pushed the door open and tripped over something lying on the floor. I picked up the object and frowned. "Speaking of Rina, she left her phone in the doorway."

"Christopher," Anya called. "You'd best come hear this."

"Who is she talking to over there?" Maisie asked.

"Long story. Rina! Rob?" When there was no answer, I checked Rina's bedroom and then the bathroom. Lastly, I poked my head into my room, thus verifying that the cottage was empty.

"They must have gone out," I said.

"Christopher," Anya yelled. "Quickly, please!"

"Excuse me," I mumbled. I left Maisie complaining in the doorway as I ducked into the herd of wights. "What's up?" I asked Anya.

"They're saying your sister's name," Anya replied. The wights were buzzing around Anya's head while they chirped and chittered. "They're speaking too fast and I can't hardly understand them, but they keep saying Mistress Stewart."

"What's this about Rina?" I demanded, and the wights chirped louder. "Do you know where she is?"

"Calm down, the lot of you," Anya said. "I need you to slow down so I can understand what you're telling me." Before Anya could figure out what was going on with Rina or the wights, Rob came striding down the lane carrying two market bags.

"Glad to see the both o' ye," Rob called as he walked toward us. "Just returned, have ye?"

"Yeah." I looked behind him. "Rina isn't with you?"

"She's not. She stayed behind to rest."

Suddenly, I felt like the ground had fallen away beneath my feet. "Rob, she's not here."

"What d'ye mean no' here?" Robert shoved past Maisie as he entered the cottage. "Karina!"

"Master Kirk, that's what we've been trying to tell you all," Wyatt said, as he hovered in front of Robert. "Mistress Stewart has been abducted."

The bags fell to the floor as Robert's armor materialized on his body. "Tell me everything ye saw."

CINNABAR

I was moving. In a car?

I was on fire.

Hot hot hot...but cold.

So cold...

I shivered and shuddered, then the fire erupted in my chest and I couldn't breathe.

Everything went dark.

I woke up lying face down in the back seat of a vehicle I didn't recognize, covered in cold sweat and retching. Something had given me terrible heartburn, and that, coupled with the motion of the car, made for an epic bout of nausea.

I wiped my mouth on my sleeve and tried to sit up. I got as far as propping myself up on my elbows, but that was all the altitude I could handle before my stomach protested. I laid down on my side and positioned myself so I could see who was driving this strange car.

Shit. John was driving.

"Where are you taking me?" I croaked, my throat raw. "Why am I sick?"

"Don't get too sick, now," he said. "Empty all of it out of your belly and I'll just give ye more."

Panic squeezed my heart. "More of what?"

"Just a little potion I brewed up especially for ye." He glanced back at me. "It will enhance your natural ability to create portals. Isn't that a good thing?"

"John. What was in that potion?"

"Ye are an alchemist, or so ye claim. Figure it out."

I moved onto my back and stared at the car's ceiling, mentally cataloging every alchemical compound and elixir I'd studied. Western alchemy—which was most likely what John had learned, originally at least—was mostly concerned with transmuting base metals, like lead, into gold. Mercury was also often used in the process. Lead and mercury were poisonous even in small amounts, which did not bode well for me or Faith.

However, I couldn't reconcile how lead, gold, or mercury could help me create an interdimensional portal. I thought about other alchemical traditions, and recalled that in Indian lore the aim is to create divine immortality within a mortal body. Those recipes also called for mercury, and it was mixed with sulphur. Practitioners of Chinese alchemy used mercuric oxide to commit a form of ritual suicide.

What are the symptoms of mercury poisoning? I was experiencing tremors, anxiety, and nausea, but that could be due to a hundred other reasons. Not to mention that mercury needed time to build up in one's body before any symptoms presented, and according to the clock on the dashboard, I hadn't been with John for very long. But I had that telltale mercuric flavor of clean metal in my mouth, and the whole car stank of brimstone, or rather, sulphur.

Mercury and sulphur... Those two elements were part of the Islamic elemental system, the other five being aether, air, fire, water, and earth. Perhaps if a certain element was increased in one's body, it would make one more susceptible to slipping between worlds...

"Did you try to increase my air?" I asked. When he tossed a sly glance over his shoulder I knew I was on to something. "Aether?"

He laughed. "Perhaps ye did learn somethin' at than fancy university across the sea." He turned his attention back to the road, and ignored me for a time. Eventually, he said, "Fire."

"Fire?" I propped myself up on my elbows. "Did you use powdered sulphur on me? Is that why everything smells like matches?"

"And what is the symbol o' sulphur?" he asked.

"A fire cross," I mumbled.

John took a corner at high speed, and my stomach roiled. I bent over and retched onto the car's floor. When I wiped my hand over my mouth, my fingers came back red, but not with blood.

"Cinnabar," I whispered, noting the dark red hue and the acrid stench of brimstone. He'd either blown powdered cinnabar—which was a naturally occurring form of mercuric sulfide—into my face or he'd liquefied it and poured it down my throat. I mentally ran down the list of sulphur toxicity symptoms: respiratory irritation, chemical burns, muscle cramping, and in extreme cases, swollen lungs leading to permanent airway damage.

Holy shit, John might really mean to kill me.

"Is your plan to fire up my spirit and set it free?" I asked. "Send my soul flying across the dimensions and flinging open portals in its wake?"

"Ye really do no' ken all that much about your natural ability," John said, shaking his head. "'Tis a pity. The Stewarts were once the most sought after walkers in the land."

"It's genetic?" I asked. "Wouldn't that make you a walker?"

"While it does typically appear in the males o' the line, my predilection was more for the magical arts," John replied. "'Tis why I kept abreast o' what your brother was up to."

"You thought Chris was a walker?"

"I did, but as with me, his talents lie elsewhere."

Interesting. "Why did you imprison the giants?"

"What giants?" John asked. "I ha' ne'er imprisoned a giant in all my days."

"Beira—the Cailleach Bheur—sent Chris to free a giantess called Long Meg. Beira said that you had imprisoned her."

John laughed as if I'd just told him the funniest joke in the world. "I did no' such thing. A wizard called Scot imprisoned her and a score o' her friends hundreds o' years before I was born. But let me ask ye this, Karina dear. Why would Beira want Christopher to run pell mell across the countryside to be freein' a stand o' giants?"

I had no idea what Beira wanted with giants, but my raw throat put me off asking any more questions. I flopped back onto the seat, and heard the tiniest screech near my ear. I moved so my head was directly behind the driver's seat and picked a lavender wight—the one who had cared for my African violet all the months I'd been away in New York—out of my hair.

"Can you get back to the cottage?" I whispered, and she nodded. "Go to Robert and tell him where I'm headed, and with who."

Louder, I asked, "Can you crack a window? This smell is killing me."

"Stop puking, then," John said, but he hit a button and one of the rear windows slid down an inch or so. The wight touched my cheek, then she flew out of the window and was gone.

I hope she flies fast.

TAKE THE TRUCK, AND THE TOOLBOX

Anya, Robert, Maisie, and I were standing inside the cottage, the front door flung wide open as the wights swarmed inside and back out to the garden again. Most of them had seen John take a dark red powder out of his coat and blow it into Rina's face. Rina had collapsed, then John loaded her into the back of a car and drove away. Some had tried following, but cars could move a lot faster than a wight's tiny wings could fly.

Throughout it all, Robert was as still as a statue, his arms crossed over his chest and his gaze hard as stone. Anya flitted from one wight to the next, asking questions in their chirping language and translating it to English, while Robert absorbed every last piece of information she conveyed. I almost felt bad for John.

On second thought, no, I didn't.

"What are they doing?" Maisie asked, and I remembered that she couldn't see the wights. "Performance art? And is he supposed to be a knight?"

"Ah, you wouldn't believe me if I told you," I said.

"Try me," Maisie challenged.

"Christopher," Robert growled. "The cupboard next to the toaster."

"Okay." I went directly to the cabinet and opened it. The cupboard was bare except for a glass jar filled with a waxy substance flecked with dried herbs.

I wheeled around and demanded, "You want me to put fairy ointment on my agent?"

"She's in it, she may as well see it," Robert replied.

"She's not in anything! She's just standing here!"

"What am I in?" Maisie asked. "Chris, what have you gotten into this time?"

I took a deep breath and pinched the bridge of my nose. "Here," I said, and set the jar in her hands. "Put that on your eyes and you'll see fairies. Gods, too. Have fun."

Maisie scrutinized the jar, then she unscrewed the lid and smelled the contents. Since she was occupied for the moment, and there wasn't anything else useful for me to do, I grabbed the fallen grocery bags and set about putting the food away. I laughed in spite of everything when I saw what Rob had purchased; eggs—which luckily hadn't broken when they'd been dropped—orange juice, oatmeal, a bar of dark chocolate, a pound of coffee, and three jars of olives. Based on this grocery haul, Rina and Rob were made for each other. In the midst of my domestic duties, I saw a black-and-white photograph lying on the counter.

Who prints photos these days? I picked it up, marveling at the very thin, very shiny paper. The picture itself was a swirl of gray and black, like some kind of organic abstract art.

"What is this?" I asked. Anya and Robert both stopped talking and stared at me, since a random photo was the least of our worries. "This picture, it's just strange. I've never seen anything like it."

Robert looked at the photo in my hand, and his face crumpled. "That is an image o' me bairn, Faith. The doctor referred to it as an ultra sound."

"Oh." I was holding a picture of my niece. Goddamnit, this will not be the only time I ever hold her.

"Is someone pregnant?" Maisie asked. I looked up and saw shiny blobs of ointment smeared around her eyes. Great.

"Yes. My sister," I said.

"*Mazel tov*. So those two are talking to butterflies?"

Anya walked toward the fireplace and ran her fingers across the shelf that rested above it. The only item on the shelf was Rina's ammonite fossil. "Where is the cornucopia?"

A lavender wight flew in through the front door at near-supersonic speed. It circled the room twice before landing on Anya's shoulder. It chirped in her ear for a moment, then Anya picked it up and held it between her and Robert.

"This one went with Karina," Anya said. "Hid in her hair, she did, brave little lass."

"Where are they?" Robert demanded. The wight chirped, and Anya nodded.

"They're going to Glen Lyon," Anya announced.

"The wight told you that?" I asked.

"Based on their direction and how long they've been driving, it's my best guess," Anya replied. She glanced at me, then back at Robert. "Glen Lyon is a favorite place of my mum's."

"Is Beira involved in this?" Robert's voice was soft, but it carried the promise of how he would deal with those responsible for taking Rina from him.

"She is, but I'm not sure to what degree," Anya replied. "Robert, if I ever thought she might harm Karina and the bairn—"

Robert made a cutting motion with his hand. "We'll concern ourselves with who is ultimately responsible for this later. We need to get Karina away from that madman first." Robert turned toward me. "Can ye locate a map, and drive us to Glen Lyon?"

"Hang on." I punched the place name into my phone's GPS. "Shit. It's three hours west."

"How long has he had Karina?" Robert asked the wight. As it chirped and flailed its tiny arms, the cottage's caretaker, Dougal MacKay, appeared in the doorway.

"Take me truck," Dougal said.

"Does it travel at the speed of light?" I asked. "If it doesn't, I'm sure my car is faster."

"When driven wi' purpose me truck can get ye anywhere ye need to be. It e'en helped this fool drive home after his last adventure," Dougal added with a nod toward Robert.

"Can we trust this truck?" Anya asked. "No offense, but I cannot even trust my own right now."

Dougal nodded. "No offense taken. Ye all go on now, before the walker ends up in dire straits."

With that, Dougal left. Since we didn't need any more random people wandering into the house, I walked over and closed and locked the front door. "All right, we need to get to Glen Lyon. We're going your way?"

"We are." Anya took my hand, then Robert's, and we blinked out. A second later, we were back in the cottage.

"Whoa," Maisie said.

"What the bloody hell was that?" Robert roared.

"The glen is warded," Anya said. "Against the both of you!"

"Is it warded against you?" I asked.

"No."

I ran my hand through my hair. "Go to Rina. I'll get Robert there as fast as I can."

Anya nodded and blinked out. I grabbed my car keys, then thought the better of it. My car wasn't registered or insured, and the last thing we needed was to get stopped on the way by Scotland's finest.

"Should we take Dougal's truck?" I asked. "It might be our best option."

"Aye." Robert grabbed a toolbox that was stting on the floor near the coffee table. "And I'm bloody well takin' his tools with me, too."

GLEN LYON

E ventually, the car stopped moving, which my stomach and raw-from-puking throat thought was just great. I don't normally get carsick to such an extent, but then again, I'd never been kidnapped and poisoned while pregnant before.

I rubbed my bump and gave Faith a silent pep talk. Robert and I had both drunk that life and health enhancing elixir supplied by Fionnlagh several times now, and Anya had told me it should positively affect Faith as well. However, Anya was no chemist, and I still didn't know what was in the potion that conveniently appeared in Robert's armored coat every few weeks. No matter what was in those little bottles, it clearly didn't afford any extra protection against poison. I wondered if it was doing anything to protect Faith.

"Stay with me, girl," I whispered. "I'll get us out of this."

John opened the back door and grabbed my arm. "Holy hell, it stinks back here," he said.

"Poison makes you vomit," I rasped. "Body's first line of defense."

He pulled me out of the car and to my feet, and put his arm around my upper back as he helped me walk. Despite me dragging my feet, my legs were working just fine, but I wanted to hinder John as much as possible. Robert must have returned to the cottage by now, and I knew he'd be searching for me. Hopefully, the lavender wight would get to him soon.

I also wanted to get a good, long look at my surroundings. We were in a valley, and John had driven right to the end of the only paved road in sight. On one side of the valley was a hydroelectric dam, and we followed a narrow trail that skirted the edge of a lake. After about thirty minutes of walking, the trail moved away from the modern structure and deeper into the forest. Based on the sun's position overhead, I thought we were going west. I was certain that I had no idea of where he'd taken me.

And so we went, John dragging me along the trail until I wasn't acting exhausted and he really was dragging me. He kept hold of me the entire time we walked, but it hardly mattered. Even if I'd had the strength to get away from him, I didn't know which direction would lead me to safety.

The trail inclined upward, as all trails eventually do in Scotland, and we left the woods for a massive plain nestled between two mountains. We trudged across that flat yet harsh terrain, until we reached a tiny house comprised of three stacked stone walls and a sod covered roof. The front of the house was open, and the interior was packed with a dozen or so rocks that were so smooth they must have been dredged up from a river.

"This your rock collection?" I asked. It was the first time I'd spoken since John had dragged me out of the car.

"No. Hers." I followed his gaze, and saw Beira standing just beyond the tiny house.

The Queen of Winter—because she was standing there as a queen, not as the bartender of the village pub—was wearing a fitted high necked shirt and matching pants, both in the pale bluish hue of icebergs, topped with a gray fur cloak. The pants were tucked into tall white boots that were immaculately clean, which told me she hadn't stomped through the muddy field to get here. In her left hand she held a white metal staff, and chains of pink and blue flowers decorated her hair, along with a crown made from shards of ice. Standing behind her were more than a dozen giants, and I was betting Long Meg was one of them.

As I took in Beira's obvious display of power, I understood two things: I knew who was behind the Wild Court, and that Beira was not there to help me.

"I've brought ye the walker, mistress," John yelled. He released his hold, and I crumpled to the cold, hard ground. There was some grass present, but it had yellowed over the winter and wasn't much of a cushion.

Beira rushed to my side and helped me sit up. "Karina, what has happened to ye?" she asked.

"He poisoned me." Beira put a hand on either side of my face, and her impossibly bright blue eyes stared into mine. "Can you help me? I-I don't know if the poison will hurt my baby."

"O' course I will help ye," Beira said. "But I do need a bit o' help from ye as well."

"Okay." The cold from the ground was seeping into my bones, and I started shaking. Or maybe that was from the poison, who knew. "Why did you say my uncle imprisoned Meg? John said it was someone else."

"Was I mistaken? Happens to the best of us. Up with ye, now." Beira helped me stand up, and supported me as we walked over to the stone house. "Ye ken how ye are more concerned with your bairn than e'en your own life?"

"Yes."

"These stones aren't just stones. They are me family." She caressed one of the boulders and smiled. "They call this one the Bodach. 'Tis me husband in there. The rest are our sons, all fine, strong lads."

"Wow. Did the same person imprison them that imprisoned Meg?"

Beira shook her head. "Nay, 'twas a different man. For a time, wizards earned their coin by charging mortals to quell giants in such a manner, and then having us pay to have our loves released. That was how Meg and hers were trapped. 'Twas a right awful scheme, but things went as such for eons."

"But someone else went after your family?"

"A punishment is what they faced." Beira fell silent, stroking the top of the boulder that contained her husband. "When it happened, I was distraught, but not overmuch. After all, my man and boys are safe where they are. I assumed I would bide me time, and once things had calmed down, I would have them released and all would be well. Then magic pulled back from the natural world and most of me family was trapped."

"I'm sorry. That's horrible."

"It was, and it is, but lucky for me, ye can help me get them back."

"Me? What can I do?"

Beira put her hands on my shoulders and held me at arm's length. "I need ye to open a door, and lead me back to the home that was once mine. There I can access enough power to free me family."

"I thought you lived at the pub," I said, playing dumb and stalling for time.

"I once had me own court, did ye ken?" she asked. "I truly was the Winter Queen, and lived half the year in a castle made of ice so clear it shone like glass. Me palace was shattered by those who worked against me and imprisoned my boys, but no matter. I can rebuild. We can always rebuild."

"H-How can I help? I don't know how to build anything."

"I just need ye to open a door to the Winter Court, so I may gather what I need."

I felt my muscles spasm in the back of my legs and near my spine. "I don't really know how to make a door. I'm still new at this."

"I will help ye." Beira slid her hands down to mine. "Listen to me, and do what I say."

My abdomen cramped so hard tears spilled down my cheeks. I loosened my hands from Beira's and shoved them inside my hoodie's front pocket, and felt the crunched up basket inside. "If I do what you ask, will you save my baby?"

Beira gave me what I'm sure she thought was a motherly smile. "O' course, love."

Before anything more could happen,, Anya appeared next to us. If I hadn't felt so sick I would have had a heart attack. "Mum! What are you doing here with Karina? The gallowglass is in a state."

"We need her," Beira hissed. "Ye ken that well, don't ye?"

"No, Mum, I don't," Anya said. "Can't you see that she needs help?"

"We need her to open a door to the Winter Court!" Beria snapped.

Anya's eyes widened and she took a step back. "No, Mum, that's forbidden. Karina, you cannot do this."

"Me own flesh and blood betrays me," Beira shrieked.

"It's okay." I touched Beira's arm. "I'll do it."

"Karina," Anya began, but I shook my head.

"Anya, I need help," I sobbed. "John poisoned me, and if I open a door, Beira will reverse it."

"Poison?" Anya's gaze few toward my middle, and she saw the odd-shaped lump in my front pocket. "What have you got in that pouch?"

"Enough, lass," Beira snapped, then she turned back to me and grinned a terrifying, toothy grin. "Now then, Karina, do as I say. Begin by closing your eyes."

I did, and Beira explained to me what the Winter Court had looked like in its prime: a palace of ice as hard and clear as diamonds, sweeping lawns covered in thick blankets of white snow, and everything inside and out was clear and cold and sparkling. Once she was satisfied that I understood where and what the Court was, she began instructing me on how to visualize a portal inside my mind and bring it to life.

"Karina, you already have everything you need," Anya yelled. "Next to Faith, everything you need."

My brain was focused on Beira's voice, but my hands were in my front pocket, right over my belly. Instinctively I flexed my fingers, and closed them on a magical artifact I'd almost forgotten about.

The cornucopia.

"Antidote," I said aloud. "Cornucopia, I need an antidote."

Beira stopped her mantra and asked me what I was talking about as I withdrew a glass bottle from the cornucopia. I stepped back from the Queen of Winter, pulled out the cork, and drank.

Holy shit, the antidote was as bad as the poison. I could feel it coursing through me, like lava flowing through my veins and searing into my bones. Was the antidote burning the poison out of me, or just poisoning me in a different manner? I stumbled backward, certain I was going to collapse. Then the flames ebbed into a gentle warmth, and pooled in my belly. In my mind's eye I saw Faith, but not how she'd looked on the ultrasound machine. I saw my baby well and whole and happy, and surrounded by spring flowers.

We were okay. Faith and I were okay.

"Thank you, Persephone," I whispered.

I opened my eyes. Beira was as still as stone, and a frosty rime covered her skin. "Are ye feelin' better, then?" she asked.

"Yes." I stashed the bottle in my pocket. "I will still help you. I promised I would open a door, and I'll do it."

"Karina," Anya shrieked.

"A sense o' duty and obligation is a fine trait. A shame I couldn't impart that on me own daughter." Beira turned her back on Anya and faced me. "Now, love, just do as I told ye."

"All right."

I closed my eyes and pictured the doorway to a fairy court, but not the one Beira had described. Instead of visualizing an icy palace guarded by wolves and giants, I drilled a hole from this dimension right through to the Seelie Court, then I pulled Fionnlagh and Nicnevin through the portal and deposited them right in front of us.

The Seelie King and Queen stared at me for a moment, then they fixed Beira in their gazes.

"Cailleach Bheur," Nicnevin said. "How perfectly awful to see you."

FATE

As soon as Anya had teleported out of the cottage, Robert and I ran to Dougal's truck. The keys were already in the ignition, which was a nice bit of luck. Rob claimed the passenger seat, set the toolbox on the floor between his feet and held his sword vertically between his knees, point down. I did not remind him to buckle up.

When I opened the driver's door, Maisie slid by me and climbed into the back seat. "I don't think it's a good idea for you to come with us," I said.

"I did not fly all the way here to get left behind," she huffed.

"You might die," I said. "These are actual monsters, Maisie. Rob's sword is real."

"Drive," Rob growled. "Now."

"Well, Maisie, you're an adult," I said as I got behind the wheel and started the engine. "Coming along is your choice."

She was silent as we pulled away from the cottage. I glanced in the rearview mirror and saw her gazing at the garden wall.

"Were those really fairies?" she asked.

"Yeah."

"They're so pretty."

I pulled onto the main road. "Now is a great time for you to tell me why you're here."

"I'm here to save your career," she snapped. "Have you read the contract for *Second Best Bed*?"

"Been a little busy," I snapped back. "Isn't this contract the same as all the others?"

"No. Those contracts were fair. This contract is a total rights grab, and it has paragraphs of shady wording."

"Since I haven't signed it yet, I imagine we can still negotiate all of those details."

"Normally yes, but there's a clause stating that if you accept any of the publisher's edits, the contract is considered valid," Maisie said. "And since you have been emailing your editor directly, who knows what else you've done!"

"Hey, they emailed me first," I said. "And I haven't gotten any edits yet, so we're good. Right?"

"Wrong."

"Christopher, Miss Perkins," Rob began, "while I do appreciate your worries for the health o' Christopher's career, rescuing me bride is my sole concern. I would appreciate silence a bit more, from the both of ye."

Wisely, Maisie and I quieted down.

A short time later, the GPS on my phone pinged, signaling a trip update. I glanced at it, and saw that even though we'd only been driving for about twenty minutes, we were almost halfway to Glen Lyon.

"This truck is fast," I said. "Supernaturally so."

"Aye," Robert said. "When I drove us home from Doon Hill, we made the journey in little more than an hour."

"That's less than half the time it took us when we first came to Crail from Aberfoyle," I said. "Wait, you drove? When did you learn how? And how did you get a license?"

"Christopher. Not now." Rob's tone brooked no argument. I looked over the dashboard, and hoped this truck knew what it was doing.

"May I ask what happened while Anya and I were in Cumbria?" I ventured.

"We went to your blasted uncle's house for dinner," Rob began, still staring forward. "He went on about how he and Karina are so much alike, the both o' them bein' alchemists and scholars and whatnot. Scared Karina half to death, though she wouldn't admit it at the time. Then we went to Doon Hill to close the door in the Minister's Pine, and learned that your uncle is the one creatin' this new court. He tried to abduct Karina then, but she ran from him."

"John's more of a liar than you realize," I said. "Meg—the giantess we freed—had never heard the name John Damian. Neither had any of the other giants, either."

Rob looked at me. "Other giants?"

"Yeah. There were a dozen or more imprisoned in a graveyard. Anya and I, uh, set them loose. Literally."

Rob grunted. "Of all the people we are acquainted with in Scotland, who keeps company with giants?"

"Everything points to Beira." I steered the truck through a twisty stretch of road. Nice to know it needed me for some of the driving. "Anya came to the same conclusion. Rob, she's not involved in whatever Beira's mixed up in."

"I believe that. Your Anya is a good one."

"Thank you."

"Ye are thankin' me for seein' the good in her?"

"You might be the only person in Scotland who could actually kill her, so yes, thank you for seeing that good."

"I do no' make a habit o' killin' those who ha' no' wronged me."

"What about Beira?" I pressed. "You're always talking about fate, and destiny. Is the gallowglass's fate to kill the Queen of Winter?"

Rob's head drooped, and he rubbed his eyes. "Bloody hell, I hope not. Ye think this is easy for me, to wear this armor and be right back in the thick of it again? All I want is to live me life and take care o' Karina and our children."

"Children? Is she having twins?"

The gallowglass smiled. "Say that to your sister and she may strike ye."

"Chris, why aren't you writing about this?" Maisie asked. I'd forgotten she was back there. "Screw Shakespeare. Readers will eat up this Queen of Winter shit."

I laughed softly. "When we find Rina, we'll ask her what I should write about."

"Aye," Rob said. "*When* we find her."

WINTER'S TEETH

T he five of us were standing in a close circle: me, the Seelie King and Queen, and the Queen of Winter and her daughter. A few yards back, the giants kept a watchful eye on us shorter ones. John had taken the middle ground between us and them. And what a motley crew we were.

Fionnlagh took a step toward me, and demanded, "Why have you brought us here?"

"Beira's behind the Wild Court," I said in a rush. Beira advanced toward me, but Anya blocked her path. "I closed the door on Doon Hill, but she wants me to make another one. She wants to go to a... a palace. An ice palace."

"She's arranged to set a stand o' giants loose as well," Anya added, nodding toward our watchers.

"How dare you betray me," Beira shrieked. "Where is your loyalty?"

"You used me and Christopher," Anya yelled. "You used his love for me as a means to an end! You lied to us, to me! How is that loyal?"

"How," Beira repeated. "I'll show ye how, ye ungrateful runt."

Beira raised her arms, and a small, icy tornado swirled around us. Her high-pitched keening threatened to shatter my eardrums, but the other three appeared unaffected. I covered my ears and squeezed my eyes shut, wishing I could open a portal back to the cottage. Either being a walker didn't work that way, or I didn't know how to open a set of doors within the same plane.

When Beira lowered her arms, the entire hilltop was blanketed with a fresh coat of show. The giants had also moved closer to us. A lot closer.

"The Winter Court will return," Beira said to Fionnlagh and Nicnevin. "I will once again rule half the year, as I was always meant to."

"You never limited your rule to six months, which is why you were punished," Nicnevin snapped. "You started off simply enough; an autumn snow squall one year, ponds and streams that remained frozen late in spring the next. But then, you and yours have always sought dominion over everything. It's why *they* were imprisoned."

Nicnevin nodded toward the stones Beira had claimed were her husband and sons. "How were you not turned to stone?" I whispered to Anya.

"I was very young when it happened." Anya surreptitiously took my elbow. "Hold tight, walker."

Anya blinked, and we were gone from the clearing. I knew it happened, felt us leave the glen... Then an icy claw wrapped itself around us and hauled us right back.

"You do not leave without my say," Beira yelled, as I grabbed onto Anya to keep from falling. Beira slammed her staff into the ground as she pointed at me. "You three can go. The walker stays."

"She does no' belong with ye!"

Tears sprung from my eyes at the sound of his voice. I twisted around and saw Robert stalking toward us, his sword out and sunlight gleaming off the wickedly sharp edge. Chris—and his agent?—were scrambling across the field behind him.

"Ye have no business with Karina," Robert yelled. "I demand ye leave her be."

Beira laughed, then she crouched and thrust her arm forward. Anya, Fionnlagh and Nicnevin were thrust away from her as I was drawn to her side. A wall of ice grew up and around us, creating a frozen dome that trapped me and Beira inside with the giants. The Queen of Winter showed me her teeth.

"Let's talk, just you and I," Beira said.

BOTH SIDES OF THE SEELIE

As the three of us reached the crest of the hill, Beira waved her hand. Suddenly, Anya and the Seelie King and Queen were standing next to us, and Beira was clutching Rina's arm. Then a set of ice walls erupted from the bare earth and climbed at least twenty feet into the air, separating us from Rina, Beira, and Beira's gang of giants. Giants that Anya and I had set free. The ice walls were so thick they were opaque, and we couldn't hear anything from the other side.

Robert ran around and behind the walls, and came back around a moment later. "Blasted ice is closed," he yelled, then he kicked the ice. "She's imprisoned Karina with her!"

"What is that?" Maisie asked. "One of those ice hotels?"

"No, Maisie, the Queen of Winter is using it to hold my sister captive," I said. "Please wait in the truck."

"But, Chris," she protested. I was already walking away from her and toward Anya.

"I tried to get Karina away from her," Anya said. Robert was at the edge of the dome, yelling and beating the ice with the hilt of his sword.

"We teleported as one away from the glen. Mum grabbed us from the aether and yanked us back to her feet."

"Beira has finally gone mad," Fionnlagh said.

"No, she has been mad for some time," Nicnevin corrected. "Many think the loss of her family drove her over the edge, but her mind was gone long before then. Wasn't it, Anya?"

Nicnevin turned toward Anya and me and smiled. My blood went cold, but I resisted the urge to run. Rina needed me with my wits about me, not cowering from one evil woman. "Why does Beira need the giants?" I asked no one in particular. "Isn't she powerful enough on her own?"

"Protection is my guess," Fionnlagh replied. "If she is creating a new court, she will need enforcers."

"Is she creating anew, or rebuilding what was lost," Nicnevin mused. "If her aim is to have Karina transport the lot of them to the Winter Court, she'll need the giants to help uncover the castle."

"Why would Beira need help getting to her own court?" I whispered to Anya.

"It's no longer of this world," Anya replied. "It's why she needs your sister. The palace itself is inside the hollows of Beinn na Caillich, but the magic has long since been purged. When my father and brothers were set in stone, the court was nudged to an in-between place. It's not here on this plane, and nor is it in Elphame. Then they set off an avalanche to bury what was left of our home, and here we stayed."

"What the hell did your mother do?" I asked.

Anya set her jaw. "It was my da what made the offenses, and I will tell you at another time. Right now, our concern is Karina and her bairn."

Nicnevin spun around and faced Anya. "Bairn?" she repeated. "Karina is with child?"

"Aye," Anya replied. "John Damian has already poisoned her, but Karina drank an antidote given to her by the Olympian's cornucopia. Still, I fear for her."

"Poison?" I repeated. "Anya, we need to stop Beira."

Anya nodded. "Aye. We do, but few are strong enough to offer a real threat to her."

Nicnevin considered Anya for a moment, her lips pressed in a thin, bloodless line. "Robert," Nicnevin called as she moved toward him. "Allow me to assist you."

Rob paused in beating the ice, his claymore still aloft as he regarded the woman who'd held him captive for three hundred years. "Assist me how?"

"In rescuing your walker," she replied. "Your sword isn't strong enough to break Beira's magic, all because you only serve part of the Seelie Court. Pledge yourself to me as well as my husband, and you'll be strong enough to break through the ice, and deal with whatever else Beira has wrought."

Robert's gaze darted from Nicnevin to Fionnlagh and back again. "I will no' wear that collar again."

"No collar," Nicnevin said. "I swear it."

Robert nodded. "I'll hold ye to that."

"As will I," Fionnlagh added.

"Very well," Nicnevin said. "Bring your sword to me."

Robert did as she asked. Nicnevin placed both of her hands around the hilt, on top of Robert's. After a moment, Fionnlagh placed his hand on Nicnevin's. An orange glow reminiscent of Nicnevin's hair when it caught the light coated the blade and sparked off the tip.

"It is done," Nicnevin announced as she and Fionnlagh released the sword. "Go get your walker."

Robert nodded his thanks, then he turned and rushed toward the dome, bellowing a war cry as he struck the ice with the sword's pommel. The dome cracked. Robert drew back and plunged his sword into the ice up to the hilt, dragging the blade through the frozen wall like a hot knife through butter. From inside the dome I could hear the giants scream.

Nothing Stops a Gallowglass

I was lying on the frozen ground, feeling my extremities going numb. In the parts of my body where my nerve endings were still intact, I was shaking and sweating from the aftereffects of the poison and the current side effects of the antidote coursing through my body. Indifferent to my discomfort was Beira. She stood over me, all malevolence and ice, with her staff pointed at my midsection. I clutched the cornucopia like a shield, and prayed my baby would get out of this alive.

"Now, lass, why did ye bring the Seelie here?" she asked.

"I thought they could help you get home." That was the truth, though I'd wanted them to help me send Beira on her way. "Aren't you Seelie, too?"

Beira laughed. I'd heard that sound once before, when I'd gone on an Arctic cruise and watched an iceberg come apart with great floes of ice sliding into the frigid ocean. That crashing noise had haunted my dreams for weeks, and now it was bubbling up from Beira's throat as she laughed at my lack of knowledge about her kind. "I was ancient before the Seelie took their first steps. I came before all o' them, even before those Olympians that tried to abuse your gifts."

"Like you're abusing me?" I demanded. "Beira, you're no different than Demeter!"

"'Tis no' the same," Beira said, shaking her head. "Your talent is fair derived from my kind. Belongs on Alba, it does, no' in some strange land across the sea. And nor does it belong bein' chained to a set o' gods what lost many o' their followers long ago. My followers have always remained with me."

I pushed myself up to a sitting position. "Why did you have my brother free the giants? Are they your followers?"

"No' my followers, but my family," Beira replied. "And families look out for their own. Meg and hers are just the beginnin' o' my army. These with us today are the best and strongest, and they will protect me from your man, should he no' see reason."

"You only rounded up thirteen giants to protect you from Robert?" I laughed. Not the smartest move when facing off with a mad and powerful queen, but I couldn't help myself. "Do you really think a few giants—or fifty or a hundred for that matter—could actually stop the gallowglass?"

Upon hearing me mention Robert, the giants glanced at each other and started whispering among themselves. "Oh, did you keep that a secret, Beira? You didn't tell them you wanted protection from the deadliest assassin in Elphame? Because the gallowglass is coming for me." I found a woman with long, matted back hair who I assumed was the leader of the giants, and asked her, "Did you meet the man that freed all of you? Christopher? He's my brother. Some way to repay him, by keeping me imprisoned here."

"Enough!" Beira swung her staff around and thrust it at me, halting it a hair's breadth from my throat. "Keep at it and your bairn will no' have a mum."

Staring at the base of her staff, I nodded. Satisfied when I remained silent, Beira thrust her staff into the earth, then she grabbed the back of my sweatshirt and hauled me upright. "Now, do as I say."

Before I could respond, there was a crash behind me. I didn't dare turn around, but the giant's yells and the fear on Beira's face told me what had happened. Robert had broken through the ice.

"Beira," Robert bellowed. "Release Karina or lose your head!"

Beira flung me around and held my back against her chest as if I was a shield, then she raised her staff. "Forward," she ordered, and the ground shook as the giants rushed toward Robert. He planted his feet and raised his sword, fearless as the mass of giants approached him.

I screamed his name, certain they were going to trample him, when at the last moment Robert moved to the side and swung at the closest giant. His sword cut through the tendons at the back of the giant's knees, toppling him to the frozen ground. The giant screamed as bright red blood spurted like a geyser from his leg. The rest stopped advancing, and a few dragged their wounded comrade away while others regrouped to the side. Then two more advanced, and Robert relieved one of his hand while he stabbed the other in her thigh.

"I can do this all day, Beira," Robert yelled over the giants' cries. "What will ye do when no one but ye stands between me and Karina?"

"You'll have to cut me down as well, gallowglass," Beira shrieked, then she sent a whirlwind of snow and ice toward Robert. The snow was so dense I couldn't see him, and for a terrifying moment I thought he'd frozen solid. Then the wind dispersed and my fears were confirmed: Robert was encased in a solid block of ice.

"No," I whispered.

"See, lass," Beira said, "no one, no' even the gallowglass, is stronger than winter's chill."

"Is he dead?" I demanded. The ice was clear, which meant I could see Robert frozen with his sword mid-swing. I choked back sobs; it couldn't end like this, could it?

Before Beira could reply, the block of ice shuddered, then it cracked. Robert twisted from his waist and readjusted his stance as bits of ice broke loose from his armor, shattering as they hit the ground. Tears of relief coursed down my cheeks, and I was certain of one thing: nothing stops a gallowglass.

"That's not possible," Beira said.

Robert rolled his shoulders as he raised his sword. "Now then, where were we?"

PRIMROSES

Rob had broken into Beira's ice dome and shattered a large portion of the walls, and was holding his own as he battled giants and an ice queen. Actually, he was doing better than that; I couldn't see Rina or Beira through the opening he'd made, but I did see the giants rush at him, and Rob defeat them one by one. When he stabbed Long Meg I thought I was going to be sick. Then Beira froze him, and my heart nearly stopped.

"He's breaking free," Anya said as she grasped my arm. Robert was twisting inside the ice, and the block was cracking. "I've never seen a mortal man withstand Mum's abilities. Nicnevin must have increased his strength tenfold."

I nodded, but didn't speak. There was no way I was going to say anything complimentary about the woman who'd once enslaved and humiliated me.

The ice broke loose and crashed around Robert's feet. Beira shouted a few orders to the giants, and the ten who could still stand rushed at Robert again. As before, he routed them without breaking a sweat.

"I can't believe we freed the giants just to get them killed," I said.

Anya swallowed hard but said nothing, and I remembered that her father was a giant. Shit, Meg and the rest might be related to Anya, too, and Rob might end up killing them in order to save Rina. Rob might end up killing Anya's mother.

"This is wrong," I said. "There has to be a better way."

"But what is that better way?" Anya asked.

A redheaded giantess bellowed a war cry and ran toward Rob. He crouched down while holding his sword upright and caught her under her leg, using the giant's momentum to vault her into the ice wall. Upon the giantess's impact, a large section of the wall broke apart, and I could finally see Rina. She was alive, which was the only good thing about that scene. Beira had her arms wrapped around Rina, with her back flush against the mad queen's chest. The top of Beira's wooden staff was pressed against my sister's throat. Rina's face was red and her eyes were bulging; intentional or not, Beira was choking her.

"We have to get Rina out of there." I turned toward the fairies who were watching Rob battle the giants as if it was a spectator sport. "Can't one of you magic Rina away from her?"

"Not while she's in bodily contact with Beira," Fionnlagh replied. "To attempt such a thing may result in one or both of them being maimed, and I do not wish to risk Karina's welfare. Our gallowglass is Karina's best hope."

I did not like that answer. What was the point of them being fairy royalty if they couldn't help my sister? I opened my mouth to say as much, but Anya touched my elbow.

"He is correct," she said. "For all that she's mad, my mum is powerful."

"There's got to be something we can do," I said.

"We must tread carefully, and Mum knows it," Anya said. "She's well aware that none of us wish to see Karina harmed. It might be her last bargaining chip."

A chorus of screams rattled what was left of the ice dome. Rob brought his sword down on Long Meg's shoulder with a sickening crack. She went down and didn't get up. When no other giants stepped forward to face him, he pointed his sword at Beira.

"Now we go," he said. "Just ye and I."

"Aye," Beira answered. She dropped Rina and flew at Rob, brandishing her staff like a sword. Rob held his ground and their weapons clashed in mid-air, the sound reverberating around the glen. They fell away from each other, panting and circling each other like wild animals. After a moment, they regrouped and rushed each other again, with neither of them gaining nor giving ground. It seemed that the gallowglass and the Queen of Winter were evenly matched.

Throughout everything that was happening, I couldn't stop staring at the flowers strewn throughout Beira's hair. There had to be hundreds of tiny pale pink and baby blue flowers all woven into delicate chains, and peeking out from underneath her icy crown. It was incongruous, the Queen of Winter prominently displaying something so un-wintery upon her person. If I'd learned anything about the supernatural, it was that everything had a meaning, right down to the smallest detail.

"Anya," I began, "why does Beira have flowers in her hair?"

"They're primroses," she replied. "One o' the first flowers o's spring. By wearing them as part of her raiment, Mum keeps her power strong, even though her season has waned."

I grabbed Anya's shoulders and kissed her hard. "Thank you. I'm sorry."

"Sorry for what?" she asked, but I was already jogging toward Rob.

"Rob," I yelled. "The flowers! Beira's strength comes from the flowers!"

Rob looked toward me, then he withdrew a dagger from his boot and threw it directly at Beira's head. My heart was in my throat, terrified that I'd been the cause of Anya's mother's death, but Rob hadn't been aiming for Beira's body. The dagger hit the center of Beira's crown and knocked it off of her head and onto the ground. As the crown fell, the chains of primroses went with it.

"What have ye done?" Beira shrieked.

Sword in hand, Rob strode up to Beira and stomped her crown to bits, then he ground the primroses into the mud underneath his heel. "Finished ye, that's what."

Rob scooped up Rina and carried her out of the ice walls and into the light; she was either unconscious or holding herself very still. I hoped she was all right. As for the walls of the dome, they were melting at an alarming rate, with tiny streams of cold water transforming the glen into a mud pit.

Anya ran toward her mother and crouched beside her. I followed, but kept back a few paces. I didn't know what other tricks Beira still had at her disposal, and I already knew she could hold a grudge for a thousand years. Fionnlagh and Nicnevin entered the remains of the dome, and I clenched my fists and resisted the urge to hide behind my girlfriend. The royal fairies glowered at Beira while the semicircle of wounded giants glanced around uneasily. I was relieved that Rob had managed to spare the giants' lives. I hoped the Seelie would, too.

"For shame, Beira," Fionnlagh intoned. "You ken well that the Bodach and his boys are being punished, and that their time isn't yet up."

"But they're my lads too," Beira wailed. "We've been apart too long! I'm being punished just as much as they are, yet I did nothing wrong!"

"Not true, Beira," Nicnevin said, waggling her finger at the Winter Queen as if she was a naughty child. "Your crime was knowing what the Bodach was about and concealing his misdeeds. Yours was a lesser crime, but a crime nonetheless. The only reason you escaped a similar fate was because our island needed you as the Winter Queen, but now there is another."

"Who?" Beira demanded. "Who could take me place? No' the likes o' you!"

"Me?" Nicnevin's hand fluttered above her breast. "Thank you for the compliment, but I don't care for the cold. I meant her."

Nicnevin pointed at Anya, and Beira dropped to her hands and knees. "No," she wailed. "Do no' do this!"

"Listen to her," Anya implored. "I cannot rule winter!"

"It is plain that Beira can no longer rule without abusing her power," Nicnevin said. "Who better than the Queen of Winter's daughter to take up her mantle?"

Anya wrung her hands. "Mum, this is not what I want."

Fionnlagh stepped between Anya and Beira. "We do not always get what we want, or what we deserve." He waved his hand, and the very tips of his antlered headdress glowed as if lit from within. Anya gasped as the ends of her hair lifted upward, as if she'd been charged with static electricity.

But it wasn't electricity. It was the entirety of Beira's power over the cold.

"I get no say in it?" Anya demanded.

"Our options are rather limited," Fionnlagh replied. "Do you refuse?"

Anya closed her eyed and clenched her fists. "No. I accept the charge."

"Very well, then." The glow dissipated from Fionnlagh's antlers. "It is done. Anya, how do you propose we deal with the rogues in your clan?"

Anya's mouth worked, then she straightened her spine and drew back her shoulders. "Your wish is to have a court as ye once did, aye?" she asked Beira.

Beira's eyes brightened. "Aye, lass, just as I've always told ye. I must rebuild me palace, and keep it safe and sound for when our family returns."

Anya nodded. "Very well. You are to return to the Winter Court, and there you shall remain until Da's punishment has ended." Beira opened her mouth, but Anya raised her arm and made a grasping motion with her hand. Beira fell silent. She'd grabbed Beira's voice out of thin air. "Meg, a word?"

Meg limped forward and knelt. "Aye, mistress?"

"You said you owed me a favor for freeing you, and I am calling it due. You and yours shall surround the Winter Court and ensure none go in or out without my say. Will you do this?"

"Aye," Meg said, and it was echoed by the other giants. "We shall do as ye bid, Queen of Winter."

"Go, then." Anya raised her hand, and Beira and the giants faded from view. "Serve me well."

Winter's chill hung in the air long after Beira and the giants disappeared. I remained standing in the remains of the ice dome, surrounded by fae royalty with my mouth hanging open.

"What just happened?" I asked. "The giants and Beira. Are they... gone?"

"Gone, yes. Dead, no," Anya replied. "When the gallowglass cut the tether that held Mum's strength to her, it was set loose in the world. His highness the Seelie King has seen fit to transfer that strength to me."

Fionnlagh strode up to Anya and me. I'd never been so close to him before. He was amazingly tall—the illusion made more so by the antlers on his crown—and he thrummed with power. I'd never felt such strength, not even when I'd been in bed with Nicnevin. Either Nicnevin knew how to conceal her true self exceptionally well, or Fionnlagh was a force to be reckoned with.

"I trust you'll wield this power well," he said. "I'd hate for you to share your father's fate."

Anya nodded. "I'll not intrude on spring, nor summer. You have my word."

Fionnlagh nodded, then he reached for Nicnevin. They grasped hands and faded from view.

"We should check on Rina," I said. "And Maisie, I bet she's freaking out." I touched Anya's hand and tried not to recoil. She was cold as a corpse.

"Are you all right?" I asked.

"I... No. No, I am not."

"What can I do?"

She closed her eyes, and sighed. "I don't know if there's anything to be done."

GOT HIS CHANCE

After Beira choked me and dropped me on the frozen ground, it took a while for me to come back to my senses. Not gonna lie, I was pretty shocked to be not dead.

The second thing I realized—after noticed I was still alive—was that I wasn't cold. Cool, yes, thanks to a breeze skating across my skin, but I wasn't shivering. It was a soft breeze, not the frigid air Beira had called up to try and freeze the life out of me. Cool was nice.

Next, I figured out that my butt was on the ground, and the rest of my body was propped up against something; I explored it with my fingertips, and felt bark. Another tree, then. Hopefully, this one didn't have any interdimensional portals hiding in the heartwood. The tree—and therefore my body—was in a patch of sunlight, and that sunlight was probably responsible for driving the last bits of cold out of my fingers and toes. Then a shadow fell across me and I flinched.

"Karina, 'tis me," Robert said. "'Tis only me."

I opened my eyes and there he was, the gallowglass who struck fear into the hearts of humans and fae alike, crouching in front of me and wearing the most worried face I'd ever seen. "Hey."

"Hey, yourself." Robert felt my forehead, then my hands. "How d'ye feel?"

"Better," I replied. "I can breathe again, and I think the antidote took care of the poison." I withdrew the cornucopia from my front pocket. "Persephone saved us again. Maybe we should have relocated to Greece."

"You're certain you're well?" he pressed. "And our bairn?"

"Faith is good." I patted my bump. "Don't ask me how I know, but she's warm and happy right now."

Robert pressed her forehead against mine. "Thank God for that."

I nodded, waiting for the lump in my throat to pass. "What happened with Beira?"

He jerked his head to the side. I saw a melting ice wall and some giant heads bobbing around above the top edge. "She's in there, with the Seelie. I divested her of a measure o' her power. Now, she's being dealt with."

"Really." I pushed myself up so I was sitting more than leaning. "How'd you do that?"

"The flowers in her hair gave her a bit o' spring. Kept her power strong when it should have waned like the season. I cut the flowers loose, and here we are."

"Huh. That was pretty smart."

"'Twas Christopher who suggested it."

"We Stewart kids are pretty brainy."

Robert brought my hand to his mouth and kissed my knuckles. "Brilliant ye are, and our bairn will be brilliant as well. Most likely as bonnie as her mum, too, and she'll have a legion of suitors beatin' a path to her door."

"I bet." I squeezed his hand a bit tighter. "What happened with John?"

"The coward turned tail and ran. But fear not me love, I am certain I will find the rogue, for I brought Dougal's tool box with me."

"Did you ask it for John's head?"

Robert snorted. "No, but only because I wish to take it meself. Instead, I asked it for a way to find him." Robert withdrew a compass from inside his coat and presented it to me. I examined it, and learned that no matter which way I turned the compass, the needle always pointed southwest.

"I guess that's the way he went," I said.

"Seems to be." Robert closed my hand over the compass. "I will find him, and ensure that he will never harm ye again. Ye have me word, Karina."

I smiled. "I know you will find him."

He smiled back. "I finally got me chance."

"Chance to what?"

"I rescued ye."

"About time." I grabbed his arm and pulled him down beside me. He wrapped his arm around my shoulder and I leaned into him. "Thank you."

"Welcome, love. But don't make me do that again."

WINTER TOGETHER

At Rob's insistence, Anya teleported him and Rina directly to a hospital. I waited—and waited—at Glen Lyon for Anya to return and give me an update on my sister, or just to talk, but she didn't. After an hour had gone by, I admitted defeat, and walked back to the truck.

Maisie was waiting at the truck, just like I'd asked her to. "I'm thinking that all of this is above and beyond your job description," I said.

"You don't know the half of it," she said.

"I can't believe you flew all the way here just to talk to me."

She shrugged. "I had frequent flyer miles."

We got into the truck, and it started up like a regular vehicle. "I suppose it's only fair for me to tell you what's really been going on," I began, and then I told her everything. I started with Olivia leaving me, and how that led to me and Rina coming to Scotland in the first place. I told her about Sorcha, who was really the Seelie Queen, and how my sister had freed the gallowglass and then marched into Elphame, ended Rob's curse, and rescued me. Lastly, I told her about Beira, and the giants, and Anya.

"Shit," Maisie said after I'd explained how my girlfriend was now the Queen of Winter. "Maybe you should ditch fiction altogether and write a memoir. *My Affair with the Fairy Queen* or something like that. Wait, I have it. *The Love That Melted the Ice Queen's Heart*."

I glanced at her. Based on her expression, she was serious. "Would anyone read that?"

"You'd be surprised what people will fall for." Maisie reached into her bag and withdrew a notebook. "Now that you've told me your story, let me tell you the story of why I'm here."

"I'm sorry I wasn't replying to you."

She held up a hand. "Water under the bridge. Anyway, to make a long story short, your publisher is ruining your reputation in the name of profits."

I snorted. "Can my reputation get any lower?"

"As it turns out, yes it can. They're marketing you as a modern day Humbert Humbert, a teacher that preys on his underage students and then makes them disappear."

"What? That's nonsense! When I met Olivia, she was twenty. School records will prove that."

"Olivia has also fallen off the face of the earth," Maisie said. "They're feeding the rumor mill, and implying that you might have offed her the way Humbert offed Dolores's mother."

"Humbert didn't 'off' Charlotte." Correcting Maisie's knowledge of twentieth century literature was easier than dealing with this fresh hell. "She was hit by a car."

"Car, schmar. My point is that they're one legal loophole away from libel, and they have enough lawyers in their pocket to stay on the right side of the law. They're controlling the narrative right now, and we need to stop them."

"How do we do that?"

"Glad you asked," Maisie replied. "First off, you do not want to sign another contract with these people."

"I haven't, and I won't."

"Good. Step two is us finding you a new publisher."

I remembered all of the rejections slips I'd gotten back when Maisie had shopped my first novel. At the time, it had been the worst experience of my life. "Will any other company want it? With all the bad PR I've gotten?"

"Of course people will want it. *Second Best Bed* is an amazing book, and *Bones of the Bard* is still on the bestseller list. Let me help you find it an amazing home at a company that will treat you the way you deserve to be treated."

"You really think it's that good?"

"I really think it's that good."

"All right, then. "I smiled, for once feeling in control of my future. "Let's do it."

As it turned out, whatever magical speed spell had been placed on the truck had worn off, and it took us over four hours to drive back to Crail from Glen Lyon. The trip would have taken much less time if Maisie's bladder was larger than a thimble and didn't force us to stop every hour.

When we got to the cottage, we found Rina and Rob sitting at the kitchen table, smiling and feeding each other olives straight from the jar. "I take it everything went well at the hospital," I said by way of greeting.

Rina jumped up from the table and ran to hug me. "I'm so glad you're okay," she said. "Anya said you were, but seeing is believing, you know."

"I know." I held her at arm's length. "Did you go to the hospital? What did they say?"

"We went. By the way, Scottish hospitals have their shit way more together than American hospitals," she added.

"And the baby?" I prompted.

"Faith is awesome. And get this—she kicked!" Rina glanced at Rob, who was sitting at the table wearing a satisfied grin. "I was lying there on the table in one of those stupid hospital outfits and all these people were rushing around and she just kicked! It was like she was saying hey guys, I'm okay."

"That is the best news I've ever heard," I said.

"I know, right?" Rina looked past me and waved. "Hey, Maisie. Sorry I hung up on you that time. We've kind of got a lot going on here."

"No worries," Maisie said. "I was just telling Chris he should write about this instead of Shakespeare."

Rina laughed. "I suppose that would be cheaper than therapy."

Everyone stopped what they were doing and stared at the front door. I turned as well, and saw Anya standing just beyond the threshold.

"Hi," I said. "I waited for you, at the glen."

"I know you did." Anya smiled tightly. "Hello. Karina, I am glad to hear you and the bairn are doing well."

"We are, thanks to you." Rina stepped back from me and returned to the table. "Are you hungry, Maisie? We have snacks."

"I love snacks," Maisie said as she took a seat.

"Walk with me, Christopher?" Anya asked.

"Yeah. Sure."

Anya and I headed across the meadow behind the cottage. The landscape was just beginning to show signs of spring, with tufts of grass and wildflowers poking through last year's yellowed turf. I remembered the primroses in Beira's hair, and wondered what Anya would do for the next few months, and after.

"I never thought of you as a princess," I said at length.

"What's that?"

"If your mother is a queen, that makes you a princess. I never made that connection until just now."

"If you didn't think of me as a princess, how did you think of me?"

"As my girlfriend. My Anya."

She smiled as red stained her cheeks. I'd just made the new Queen of Winter blush. "And now?"

"I don't know. A lot happened earlier."

She pursed her lips and gazed toward the horizon. "Aye. A lot did happen. Thank you, for your honesty."

"What will you do?"

Anya dropped her gaze, and studied the ground. "I don't need to do anything right now. Winter's over, and I'm not supposed to have influence over the land for some months yet."

"That's good. You'll have time to learn how to... To winter?"

She laughed. "Yes, I have time to learn how to winter." She paused for a moment. "In the old days, long afore the Seelie and Unseelie built their courts, there was a Winter Queen and a Summer King. Mortal enemies, they were. Winter began when Mum defeated the Summer King, and the opposite happened when summer commenced."

"Why did things change?"

"That's something else my da caused," Anya said. "He grew tired of Mum spending time with another man, even though they only saw each other twice a year, and then only to pummel each other. Da challenged the Summer King, and when he defeated him, he stripped him of his power." She offered a sheepish grin. "He was a bit of a ruffian."

"So you take after him?"

"Oh, absolutely."

We were silent for a time. Then I said, "You know, I've always liked winter best. Summer's just too damn hot, and spring pollen fires up my allergies. Winter is definitely the best season. You've got skiing, and hot chocolate, and snow makes everything prettier."

Anya cocked an eyebrow at me. "What are you saying, Christopher?"

"If you need help—not that you need help, but if you want some help—learning all about how to run winter, I'd love to help you."

"You would?" Anya said. "You don't hold against me what my mum did to Karina? How she tricked you?"

"She tricked you, too." I took Anya's hands. Unlike how she'd felt earlier, both of her hands were warm and soft, and not wintery at all. "So, what do you say? Want to learn how to winter together?"

"Aye. We shall winter together."

MORE THAN PRETTY GOOD

After all of the chaos at Glen Lyon, I'd only wanted to sleep for a week, but Robert wouldn't hear of it. He'd immediately made us an appointment at the medical center, and stood there scowling while Dr. Khanna and her assistants checked over every inch of me. When she pronounced both me and Faith as healthy as horses, Robert was so relieved he wept.

With my second clean bill of health in as many days, and a shiny new set of ultrasound pictures in hand, Robert and I then headed to the Laundromat to deal with our accumulated clothing. That trip cemented our desire to purchase a washing machine of our very own. Hauling dirty clothes around was for the birds.

Our next task was locating a builder, and figuring out what sort of addition we wanted to put on the cottage. We settled on adding a second level with two bedrooms and a bathroom, and converting one of the downstairs bedrooms into a laundry room. Yeah, baby, I was getting a washer *and* a dryer.

As for the other first floor bedroom, we were leaving it intact in case Chris ever needed it. He and Anya hadn't been around much lately, because they were spending the summer months driving across the countryside and pretending winter wasn't getting closer every day. Since no one, not even Anya, knew what would happen to her once winter began, we thought he might need to stay with us for a few months out of the year. Or maybe he'd become the Ice King. Around here, anything was possible.

Even though many things were happening in our lives, Robert and I lucked out with a few quiet days in April. One day, he went into the village to meet with the builders, and I stayed behind to enjoy my solitude. I was sitting on the garden bench, sunning myself while the wights cared for the garden. Even though it was the middle of spring, it wasn't all that warm, but I was bundled up in many layers of wool and topped with a blanket. Robert had been confident I wouldn't freeze before dinnertime, but only just.

I turned my face toward the sun and closed my eyes. I wanted to savor these last quiet days before the baby came, just me and Robert and our little house. I was imagining the two of us having picnics in the garden when I realized she was sitting next to me.

My first instinct was to scream and run, but I tamped down my fears. After what had gone down at the glen, I knew there was more to the Seelie Queen than what appeared on the surface. We sat together for a time before she spoke.

"I suppose you've been wondering why I helped you at Glen Lyon," Nicnevin said.

I cracked an eyelid. "The thought had crossed my mind."

Nicnevin smiled, then she extended her arm. A few of the wights landed on it and started weaving flower chains around her wrist. "Did you know that I was once a mortal like you?"

"No, I didn't know that," I said. "How did you end up in El-phame?"

"That is a story for another time." The wights finished the flower bracelet and moved on to Nicnevin's hair. "But I will tell you that the magics that coursed through me and changed my body from human to what I am today left me barren."

"I'm sorry."

"Don't be. It was centuries before I understood what I'd done to myself. Fionnlagh never noticed either; fae births are so rare to begin with that whenever we do have children, we need to steal a human midwife to care for us. Eventually, one of those midwives explained that as long as I remained as I was—as I still am—I will never give Fionnlagh an heir."

"Was he upset that he wouldn't have children?"

"He has children. He has heirs. I do not." Nicnevin fell silent, and studied her hands in her lap. "That is why I could not allow Beira to harm you. I would give almost anything to carry a child, feel its life grow inside me, hear its heartbeat next to mine... But for all my power, that will never happen."

Nicnevin reached for my hand, and I let her take it. That surprised both of us. "You have been given a great and wonderful gift, Karina, and I would like to give you one more. You have my word that I will never raise a hand against you and yours. You are under my protection, as are Robert and your child."

"What about Chris?"

She raised an eyebrow at me. "Always negotiating, aren't you? Very well, Christopher is also under my protection, but not Anya. I cannot offer the Queen of Winter harbor in my court."

"I suppose that's fair." I frowned. "If I thank you, will bad things happen?"

Nicnevin tightened her fingers around mine. "Normally I'd counsel against thanking one of my kind, but just this once, it should be safe."

I smiled at the Seelie Queen. "Then thank you, from me and Robert, and Chris and Faith, too. Thank you for everything."

Nicnevin patted my hand and stood. "You are quite welcome, walker. Now I must return to my court." She sashayed toward the garden gate, then stopped as if she'd forgotten something. "When the baby comes, will you present her at court?"

"Of course," I replied.

Nicnevin smiled, deep and true. "Wonderful," she said as she faded from view. "We look forward to receiving little Faith as one of our own."

Wait, what?

When Robert returned home, he found me pacing in front of the fireplace. "I think I did a dumb thing," I said without preamble.

"Och, love, you've never done a dumb thing in your life." He folded me into his arms, and I resisted telling him of the many, many bad decisions I'd made. With my luck, he would find out about all of them, eventually. "Tell me what ye did."

"Nicnevin came by while you were out."

His arms stiffened. "And?"

"And she put me, and you, and Faith and Chris under her protection." I leaned back and focused on his eyes. "That's not a euphemism for a Seelie prison, is it?"

Robert smiled and shook his head. "'Tis no', and it is a verra good thing. It means that our family is safe from the Seelie and their hijinks for as long as Nicnevin is queen."

"Oh. But you're still their champion?"

"Aye, but 'tis no matter. Whenever I am called to fight, I will defeat my foes quickly and return to you."

"I guess. You are pretty good with a sword."

"Pretty good?" He held me at arm's length, scowling. "I am more than pretty good, ye ken!"

"You're all right." I backed toward the bedroom. "Kind of quick for an old man, too."

"I'll show ye who's quick!"

Robert leaped into action and grabbed me. I squealed as he carried me into the bedroom and kicked the door shut. I loved our life here in Crail, and I could hardly wait for our next adventure.

The next adventure begins in Touch of Frost, book one of the Winter's Queen Trilogy. Grab your copy here: https://books2read.com/touc hoffrost. Keep scrolling for a sneak peek!

For more of Karina and Robert and Chris and Anya, sign up for my newsletter at https://authorjenniferallisprovost.com

Reviews matter! Please tell the world what you thought about Karina and Robert's adventures

Thank you so much! You, the reader, make all of this worthwhile.

TOUCH OF FROST

I adored Glasgow in the summer.

In truth, I adored Glasgow all the year 'round, but summer was different. The heat imbued a new vibrancy into the already bustling city, and the people responded in kind. There were outdoor concerts, and markets, and a myriad of other ways to soak up the sunlight. We still had our fair share of rain, but this was Scotland. Anyone who went out without an umbrella deserved whatever drenching they got.

Not that I'd been taking advantage of summer's lazy days. Even as the season warmed, my new affinity for the cold made itself known, loudly and often. At first I only experienced the odd chill, but before long my food cooled as soon as it was set before me, and the ice in my drink never melted. Last week Christopher and I went to our favorite coffee shop, and I froze a cup of tea with my breath. I hadn't set foot outside the flat since. Instead, I sat on the sofa, or sometimes on one of the many window seats, and watched as others lived their lives. If

I endured much more of this frigid isolation, I'd go as mad as my mother.

"Hey." Christopher sat beside me and kissed my cheek. Today I was on the front window seat watching the birds fly past our building. "It's a beautiful day. Want to go antiquing?"

"Antiquing?" He'd noticed I'd been inside for a week, and had graciously refrained from mentioning it. Until now, that is.

"You know, shopping for vintage furniture and artwork."

"Don't we already have enough things in our flat?"

"It's not about buying so much as browsing," he replied. I didn't see the point of going shopping without intending at least one purchase, but Christopher so loved the local markets. He was also trying to help me in his own kind, gentle way.

"Perhaps we could take a stroll past the university," I said. I'd been encouraging him to seek employment in his chosen field of teaching, and utterly failing. "Do you think they've looked over your credentials?"

"Whether they have or not, I doubt they do much hiring on the weekend," Christopher replied. "That's one of the reasons antiquing is the ideal Saturday activity. Afterward, we can stop by that coffee shop you like."

"Will you buy me a sweet?" I asked. "As long as it's not ice cream."

He laughed. "You got it, beautiful. No ice cream."

"Anya, what are you doing?"

"Hmm?"

I glanced up from the rime of ice I'd created on a warped glass cabinet front. We were at yet another antique market, the third we'd found that day, and Christopher was hunting for treasures amid others' cast-offs. Antiquing was his favorite weekend hobby. As for me, I preferred sleeping late, followed by a hearty breakfast.

I also preferred having control of my abilities. I hadn't meant to freeze the cabinet door, just as I hadn't meant to frost the crystal pitcher one aisle back, or ice over the lovely reclaimed stained glass window depicting Saint Mungo and the robin. The cold was flowing out of me unchecked, rolling across everything I touched and leaving scars in its wake. Here I was on the hottest day of summer, freezing everything I touched.

I heard a ping. The glass window was cracking. I had to leave this place before something horrible happened.

Christopher peeked over my shoulder at the design I'd created. "Pretty," he said. I wonder what he would say if he knew about the rest of my handiwork, scattered among the market stalls. "Have you seen anything that might be a good present for the baby?"

The babe in question was the one his sister, Karina, was due to have within a month or so. He'd already purchased many gifts for the bairn, yet he was always on the lookout for more.

"Really, Christopher, what could be suitable for a bairn here?" I gestured to encompass the lot of dusty furniture and moldering books and fabrics.

"I thought we might find a rock specimen, or maybe a fossil," he replied.

"Those sound like presents for your sister," I said, and he didn't disagree. Karina was a geologist, and her home was filled with odd rocks and stones she found in and around Crail. "I don't think you'll find anything like that in this poor excuse for a market. These aren't even proper antiques."

"How so?"

"I'm the oldest thing here."

A crooked smile that went straight to my heart. "You're bored, aren't you?"

"A wee bit," I admitted, though I was far more terrified than bored. I heard the cracks deepen in the glass behind me, and shifted so my body blocked his view of the cabinet.

"All right." He tucked my hand into his elbow, and we walked toward the exit. "What would you like to do for the rest of the day?"

"Perhaps we can take a walk?" I glanced over my shoulder, and saw rows and rows of merchants finding shattered, frozen glass strewn about their booths. One yelled something about youths vandalizing their wares, but it hadn't been a youth. It had been me.

"What's going on back there?" Christopher wondered, as he craned his neck for a better look.

"I'm sure it's nothing," I said, as I steered him away from the destruction. "I'm in the mood for a hot cup of tea. You?"

"Sounds wonderful."

I pushed the door open, ignoring the frozen handprint I left behind. I needn't have worried about Christopher noticing the handprint since there was something far more interesting in front of us. Across the street from where we stood was a flower seller. Next to the flower seller's cart were three men far out of time, easily a millennia or more. They were armed with spears and shields, wore long hair and beards, and the cloaks and short battle tunics and trews that had been common many centuries ago. I was staring at a group of Picts smack in the middle of modern Glasgow.

I turned my back to them; I didn't know if they could see through the glamour that made me appear human, and wasn't of a mind to find out. "Christopher." I glanced toward the Picts. "Can you see them?"

"I can," he replied. "Are they... Saxons?"

"Picts, I believe."

"Picts. Of course." We approached a shop opposite from the Picts, and studied their reflection in the window. "What should we do?"

"I don't know," I said. "They don't appear to be bothering anyone. Perhaps we leave them be?"

"They're carrying spears."

"Aye, they surely are. Knives, too."

"Aren't you curious as to how they got here?"

"I am curious, but I would rather observe than engage," I replied. "For now."

"What if they do something?"

Before I could answer, ten additional men easily as far out of time as the Picts appeared out of the aether. Eight of the men surrounded the Picts, while the other two stood guard on either side. Based on the oblivious people moving around these newcomers, only Christopher and I were aware of their arrival.

"Odd." I leaned closer to the window glass, scrutinizing the newcomers' reflection. They wore metal helmets with face guards that tied underneath their chins, bronze armor, and red cloaks pinned at their shoulders. In addition to spears, they carried short swords, and curved, rectangular shields. "Where do you suppose these new ones are from?"

"Oh, those guys are Roman. No doubt about it."

I glanced at Christopher. He elaborated, "See those?" He indicated the rectangular shields in the reflection. "They're called scutums. They were carried by Roman legionaries."

I blinked at the reflected men. "When were legionaries last about?"

"They were replaced by mounted cavalry in the third, fourth century." Christopher rubbed his chin. "And I don't think any legions ever made it this far north, though there is a legend about an entire company getting lost in Scotland. As you said, odd. Maybe we—"

"Wait." I touched Christopher's arm and angled myself so I was watching the thirteen strangers over his shoulder. The legionary who I assumed was their chief nodded to the Picts, then he called to his men. They formed up and marched up the hill, disappearing from view after ten measured paces. The Picts, who appeared content with whatever had been decided, ambled off in the opposite direction. I lost sight of them when they turned a corner.

"Let's grab some lunch," Christopher said a bit too loudly. Lunch was the last thing I wanted. What I did want was to know who these men were, why ancient Picts and Romans were wandering about in modern Glasgow, what their appearance foretold. I was the future Queen of Winter, I needed to know what was afoot on my island!

I turned to Christopher to say as much, and saw his bright blue eyes, his strained smile... and I capitulated. Again.

"Lunch sounds wonderful," I said. "What about that Vietnamese spot we went to a few weeks ago?"

Christopher's smile deepened. He'd been telling everyone he encountered about the summer rolls we'd had as if they'd been imbued with magic. I'd preferred the lemongrass chicken. "I like the way you think."

"Of course you do." I glanced at the flower seller, and added, "Will you go on ahead and reserve us a table? I'd like to pick up some flowers for the flat." His brow tensed, so I added, "Order me an ale?"

He brought my hand to his lips and kissed my knuckles. "Ale it is."

I watched him walk away for a moment, then I crossed the street and examined the bouquets for sale. As soon as Christopher was out of sight, I followed the Picts. When I turned the corner, I found them leaning against a brick wall as if they belonged in this city and in this time.

"Why are you here?" I demanded.

"The gods will it so," answered one wearing a heavy gold torque. "Is that not why we're all here?"

"Why are you in Glasgow? Bit out of the way for your lot," I added, nodding to their garb.

"Why do you care?" he countered.

"Glasgow is my city, and I'll not have anyone causing trouble."

He laughed. "My lady, a more powerful man than you sent us to this very place."

"More powerful than me?" Ice skated across the pavement, licked at their boots. "Are you certain of that?"

"In a few months you may be his match, but not in the height of summer."

He nodded to the other two, and they went on their way. I debated following them, but I didn't want to keep Christopher waiting too long. I went back to the flower seller, purchased a bouquet of daisies, and continued on toward the restaurant where he waited. While I walked, two thoughts kept me occupied: the Picts were sent here by someone powerful, and that individual could be a threat.

I slipped on the icy street. As I regained my footing I glanced back, and saw ice spreading across the cobbled pavement. Perhaps I was the threat to Glasgow, and the Picts were here to stop me.

They were welcome to try.

Need to know what happens next? Get your copy here: https://boo
ks2read.com/touchoffrost

GLOSSARY

Glossary

Alchemy [al-*kuh*-mee] – a form of chemistry and speculative philosophy concerned with discovering methods for transmuting baser metals into gold, finding a universal solvent, and an elixir of life.

Anya Darach – daughter of Cailleach Bheur/Beira and the Bodach.

Beinn na Caillich – a hill west of Broadford on the Isle of Skye. Its name is translated into English as Hill of the Old Woman.

Bodach [pɔt̪əx] – a trickster or bogeyman figure in Gaelic folklore and mythology. Husband of Beira.

Cailleach Bheur/Beira [kall-EE burr/BEE-ruh] – Celtic weather deity. Personification of winter. Mother of Anya.

Carson University – an institution of higher learning in Manhattan that studies sciences, liberal arts, and theoretical magic.

Christopher Stewart – an Elizabethan scholar and bestselling author, and older brother of Karina.

Colleen Worley – administrative assistant for the earth sciences division at Carson University. Karina Stewart's best friend.

Cornucopia]kôrn(y)ə'kōpēə] – a symbol of plenty consisting of a goat's horn overflowing with flowers, fruit, and corn.

Daedalus – the father of Icarus.

<u>Demeter</u> [dɪ-MEE-tər] — in Greek mythology, Demeter is the goddess of the harvest and agriculture, who presided over grains and the fertility of the earth.

<u>Dob's Linn</u> – a site near Moffat, Scotland. It is the location of the Global Boundary Stratotype Section and Point which marks the boundary between the Ordovician and Silurian periods.

<u>Doon Hill</u> – a hill near Aberfoyle, Scotland that some believe to be a gateway to Elphame. Some believe that Robert Kirk is still imprisoned in the Minister's Pine at the crest of the hill.

<u>Drakaina</u> [dra-KAY-na] — a female serpent or dragon, sometimes with human-like features.

<u>Elphame</u> [el-faym] – Fairlyand; abode of the fairies.

<u>Fairy ointment</u> – an ointment applied to a mortal's eyes that allows them to see fairies in their true form.

<u>Fash</u> [fæʃ] – to worry, trouble, or bother.

<u>Fath-fidh</u> [fath fee] – a spell to keep things close, yet hidden.

<u>Fionnlagh</u> [fin-lay] – the Seelie King.

<u>Fuath</u> [fuə] – malevolent water spirits. Their name literally means "hate" in Gaelic.

<u>Gail Berkley</u> — head of the earth sciences division at Carson University. Karina Stewart's mentor.

<u>Gallowglass</u> [gal-oh-glas, -glahs] – a heavily armed mercenary soldier. In Elphame, the gallowglass is the Seelie Queen's assassin.

<u>Geas</u> [geSH] – (in Irish folklore) an obligation or prohibition magically imposed on a person.

<u>Glamour</u> [glam-er] – an illusion that conceals flaws or distractions.

<u>Good People</u> – a euphemism for fairies.

<u>Habetrot</u> [hay-*beh*-trot] – an imp concerned with household chores.

<u>Hades</u> [hay-DEEZ] — the ancient Greek chthonic god of the underworld, which eventually took his name.

<u>Haver</u> [hey-ver] – to equivocate; vacillate.

<u>Heracles</u> [HERR-ə-kleez] — Gatekeeper of Olympus. God of strength, heroes, sports, athletes, health, agriculture, fertility, trade, oracles and divine protector of mankind.

<u>Icarus</u> – son of Daedalus. He died when he flew too close to the sun and the wax portions of his wings—constructed by his father in an escape attempt--melted.

<u>Jared St. Lawrence</u> — student at Carson University.

<u>Karina Stewart</u> – an American geology studying at Carson University. Younger sister of Chris.

<u>Ken</u> [ken] – knowledge, understanding, or cognizance.

<u>Kirk</u> [kurk] – a church.

<u>Leannan sìth</u> [leh-nan shee] – a fairy woman who acts as a muse and offers inspiration to an artist in exchange for love and devotion. In time, she siphons off all of the artist's creativity.

<u>Leprechaun</u> [lep-*ruh*-kawn, -kon] – an Irish dwarf or sprite employed in making or mending shoes.

<u>Loch</u> [lok] – a lake.

<u>Mares of Diomedes</u> — also called the Mares of Thrace, were man-eating horses in Greek mythology.

<u>Nemeton</u> [neh-*meh*-ton] – places sacred to the old Celtic religion, primarily trees but also including temples and shrines.

<u>Nessus</u> — a centaur who was killed by Heracles, and whose tainted blood in turn killed Heracles.

<u>Nicnevin</u> [nik-*neh*-van] – the Seelie Queen.

<u>Persephone</u> [per-SEH-fə-nee] — goddess of the underworld, springtime, flowers, and vegetation.

Phooka [poo-KA] – considered to be bringers both of good and bad fortune, they could either help or hinder rural and marine communities.

Robert Kirk – a minister, Gaelic scholar, and folklorist, best known for writing *The Secret Commonwealth of Elves, Fauns, and Fairies.*

Seelie Court – the home of the light or good fairies.

Sgian dubh [skeen duve] – a small, single-edged blade.

Sorcha – a woman Chris meets in a pub, and proceeds to have a relationship with.

Tantallon Castle – a semi-ruined mid-14th-century fortress in East Lothian, Scotland. It sits atop a promontory opposite the Bass Rock, looking out onto the Firth of Forth.

Teind [tend] – a tribute due to be paid by the fairies to the devil every seven years.

Transmutation Regulations – regulation passed during the Industrial Revolution limiting the practice of alchemy in the US.

Wight [wahyt] – a small, winged fairy commonly found in gardens.

William Hargill – dean of the English department at Carson University.

<<<>>>

ALSO BY JENNIFER ALLIS PROVOST

The Chronicles of Parthalan, a six volume epic fantasy (and one short story collection)

Heir to the Sun

The Virgin Queen

Rise of the Deva'shi

Pieces of Parthalan: Six All-New Stories From The Land Of Parthalan

Golem

Elfsong

Sunfall

The Copper Legacy, a four book urban fantasy:

Copper Girl

Copper Ravens

Copper Veins

Copper Princess

A duology based in the Copper world:

Redemption

Salvation

Poison Garden, an urban fantasy filled with seers, witches, and one seriously hot detective:

Belladonna

Oleander

Bleeding Hearts

Thornapple

Wolfsbane

Mistletoe

Mandrake

Gallowglass, an urban fantasy set in Scotland and New York:

Gallowglass

Walker

Homecoming

Winter's Queen, an urban fantasy set in Scotland and Elphame:

Touch of Frost

Giant's Daughter

Elphame's Queen

Merrowkin, an urban fantasy set in Ireland above and below

Merrowkin

Death's Door

Manannán's Pearl

Changes, a contemporary romance:

Changing Teams

Changing Scenes

Changing Fate

Changing Dates

About the Author

Jennifer Allis Provost is a native New Englander who lives in a sprawling colonial along with her beautiful and precocious twins, a dog that thinks she's a kangaroo, a parrot, a junkyard cat, and a wonderful husband who never forgets to buy ice cream. As a child, she read anything and everything she could get her hands on, including a set of encyclopedias, but fantasy was always her favorite. She spends her days drinking vast amounts of coffee, arguing with her computer, and avoiding any and all domestic behavior.

Find Jenn on the web here: http://authorjenniferallisprovost.com/

For up to the minute sale notifications, follow her on Bookbub here: https://www.bookbub.com/profile/jennifer-allis-provost

For exclusive content, follow her on Patreon: https://www.patreon.com/jenniferallisprovost/

Friend her on Facebook: http://www.facebook.com/jennallis

Follow her on Instagram: @jenniferaprovost

Happy reading!

MISPRINT